T0354746

The
BLACK AMPHORA
of
HALICARNASSUS

A novel by

THOMAS FILBIN

ARCHWAY
PUBLISHING

Archway Publishing books may be ordered through booksellers or by contacting:

Archway Publishing
1663 Liberty Drive
Bloomington, IN 47403
www.archwaypublishing.com
844-669-3957

ISBN: 978-1-6657-5952-6 (sc)
ISBN: 978-1-6657-5953-3 (e)

Library of Congress Control Number: 2024908835

Print information available on the last page.

Archway Publishing rev. date: 05/07/2024

"In The Belly of the Beast"

"**R**OCK, ROCK, ROCK, THE LEOPARD'S CLOCK," the sound system in the apartment above Gordon Bauer's blared out. The music was a thumping staccato while the words were more shrieked than sung. It was four o'clock in the afternoon on a perfect June day in Manhattan, and Gordon was attempting to properly knot his necktie when the noise erupted. The tenant above him was a pallid, scruffy man who slipped in and out of the building at odd hours with scarcely more than a glance of acknowledgment for anyone who saw him.

The door across the hallway opened and a deep voice shouted, "Hey, knock it off with the noise!"

The music played as loudly as before, and Gordon could hear footsteps going up the stairs. He opened his door to the width of the chain and saw his neighbor, Louis Shaboury, ascending to the next level.

"Turn it down!" Shaboury yelled, pounding three times on the door of the ostensibly deaf music lover.

Shaboury's thudding feet descended the stairs, and after that, the rest of him came into view. He was short and squat and wore baggy black trousers and a sleeveless undershirt which revealed his hairy arms, shoulders, and neck. The fuzz continued its festival of growth in his ears and nostrils, but managed somehow to stop short of his head, which was, except for a slight fringe, bald. Shaboury had dark circles under his eyes, and if he ever owned a smile, it had been stolen from him years before by the daily annoyances of urban living. He saw Gordon peering out at him then and threw up his hands in an appeal for sympathy.

"I'm going to call the cops," he said, "and you'll back me up how loud it was."

"Absolutely," Gordon said, closing his door when Shaboury went back into his own flat.

Whether he would actually call the police was unclear. When any one of the tenants reached the authorities complaining of noise, they suggested calling the building manager first, citing matters more immediately pressing. The building manager's office was downtown, and a recorded message gave callers a long list of options:

"If you are calling with a maintenance request, press one. If you are without heat or hot water, press two. If you wish to send a fax, press three. Para Espanol…"

By then complaining tenants usually gave up because the music would come to a stop about ten minutes after it had begun. Gordon's best guess was that the man was a musician who played a few songs to motivate himself before getting ready to leave for a gig.

Gordon went back to his battle with the necktie and finally got the knot right, pulled it taut, then stared at himself for a moment in the scratched and dulled mirror that was permanently attached to one wall of his bedroom. He wondered whether it was a preview of how he would look when he was old: wrinkled and nearly invisible. He wasn't tall, and his fair skin and light brown hair made no strong impression in the glass. The grayness of age would only diminish him further until he disappeared altogether.

He turned around in his two-pretending-to-be-three room flat, and six steps later stood in what posed as a kitchen; a corner with a tiny sink, a half refrigerator, and a narrow stove with two working burners and a built-in chrome rimmed clock that had stopped at seven minutes after ten.

"On V-E day," Gordon would add when describing it to anyone.

He heated some water for tea then put a spoonful of licorice root herbal mix into the small, perforated metal ball he would dangle into the old cup with the image of Socrates on it. He waited impatiently for the water to boil, longing for the soothing taste of the tea to comfort his stomach. He had eaten a late lunch a few hours earlier at Krishnamurti's Delhi Palace, a restaurant on the ground floor of his building at Amsterdam Avenue and West 121st Street, and the three buffet helpings of the incredibly spicy chicken curry, aloo mutter, and onion chutney now felt like molten lava working its way through his innards. An uncomfortable fullness was producing a slight touch of nausea, although he thought it could just as easily be nerves. He was on his way to a lecture he felt obliged to attend, but as always on such occasions, he would be reluctant to ask anything at question time which would betray what he felt was his own colossal ignorance.

When the kettle whistled and clattered, he poured the water into the cup and sat in a wooden chair at the little table he had bought at a second-hand shop on Columbus Avenue when he first came to New York. He looked out the window at the passing cars four stories below. Soon after arriving, he had stopped looking up for a glimpse of the sky: first, because it marked him as a hick, but also because he would just have to believe it continued to exist unsensed, like the falling tree in the philosophical forest. The skyscrapers that had taken his breath away in the beginning by now could only be considered as damning evidence that New York was a wonderful idea that had gotten carried away with itself. It was Babylon with a building code, or Florence without the di Medicis, making up in sheer volume what it lacked in humanity.

The music from upstairs continued to cause the walls to vibrate, and after a few sips of tea, he gathered up his jacket, walked out, and locked the door with one standard lock and a deadbolt, opting to leave a third lock open because he was afraid he would never get the sticky slide to move again from the outside. He walked down the stairs and smelled exotic food cooking, and losing the raucous music from above, heard a quiet, lilting melody emanating from an old record player in an apartment on the second floor. It sounded vaguely Balkan, but was soon lost in the sound of a woman yelling from across the hall in what he guessed was Vietnamese.

The afternoon sun cast shadows everywhere, although he thought his side of the street was shady all the time, as if the rooftops and other buildings had been constructed in a way that blocked all daylight and left his corner perpetually cool. He saw no customers through the window of Krishnamurti's, and Gordon wondered if yet another change of ownership would befall it. In his ten months in New York it had gone from Krishnamurti's House of Curry to Krishnamurti's All Indian to Krishnamurti's Delhi Palace, the lower words changing while the upper "Krishnamurti's" remained the same. At first Gordon thought they were inter-family transfers, each subsequent owner being a Krishnamurti cousin or nephew, but when the latest proprietor, a tall, blond man with a distinctly Scandinavian accent took over, he decided it was the vagaries of the restaurant business rather than the bonds of consanguinity which explained the turnovers.

On the sidewalk in front of his building, an older black woman with hunched shoulders pushed a tiny handcart.

"Can I help you up the stairs with that, Mrs. Wyatt?" Gordon asked.

"Mercy," she exclaimed, turning around and straightening up. "That sure would be a blessing."

Gordon lifted the two-wheeled contraption and carried it up the three stairs to the landing, holding the door open for her.

"Bless you, chile," she said, and took the handle from him and rolled the cart down the first-floor corridor to the studio apartment she had under the stairwell.

Gordon left a second time and headed south on Amsterdam Avenue toward Columbia University. As his downcast eyes gazed at the crushed paper cups and Styrofoam food containers in the dirty gutter, he considered for the hundredth time whether it had been a mistake to move to a city so large it was unknowable, and certainly so expensive it was unaffordable for a graduate student with only a meager fellowship.

Gordon Bauer had spent all his twenty-three years in Illinois before coming to New York the previous September. His small-town high school in Bellflower had given him an award for the highest grades in Latin, the principal mumbling something about his gifts being an avenue to "the wider world", but to Gordon at that

point, the wider world meant only Bloomington, Peoria, or perhaps
Chicago where he was accepted at Loyola University. He continued his study of the classics under the guiding hand of the Jesuits
who thought they had a recruit for the priesthood, but the joys of
translating Virgil and Homer were soon overshadowed by the thrill
of primeval sex with Jane Freymiller, a sociology major from Eau
Claire, Wisconsin who possessed wonderfully round, ample breasts
and no irritating domestic habits. He dated her for four years of
college, secure with security, no longer having to patch together a
love life out of fumbling and unsuccessful attempts with girls from
his high school. The last catastrophe of that era was spilling a full
cup of Coca-Cola all over the front seat of his father's Buick while
trying to neck with Bernadette Flanagan after the senior prom. The
kissing had gone tolerably well, but when he reached his hand to
her thigh, she screamed and threw her arms out, launching the cup
from the dashboard and spilling its sticky contents on him, her, and
the imitation leather seats. Having found Jane, he abandoned the
chase, satisfied that satisfaction lay in the absence of having to clean
up afterward or listen to anxieties worse than his own.

   After teaching Latin for a year at a suburban high school, he
realized adolescents bored him, mainly because he was still one
himself. He considered that it would be a better life if he became
a college professor, and at the badgering of Father Kottmeyer from
Loyola, Gordon applied to graduate schools in the East. He was
startled by how well he did on the Graduate Record Examination
and was convinced he got someone else's grade when the letter of
acceptance came from Columbia.

   "Vestis virum facit, Gordon," Father Kottmeyer chortled with
glee on the telephone, the sound of ice cubes clinking in a whiskey

glass in the background, "and clothes do make the academic man: in this case the gray gown of a Columbia scholar that might enhance our classics department someday."

Gordon gulped his misgivings. "I'm not sure I want to live in New York," he told the priest as his sweaty hands fondled the letter.

"And wise you will be if you don't," the priest agreed, "at least not longer than necessary. Consider it a port of call for a few years until you are Doctor Bauer. Herr Doktor Bauer; I like it."

Gordon's parents were so overjoyed that his father sold some of the company stock he owned, having acquired it week by week through payroll deductions as manager of the household appliance department in the Bloomington store of Home Palace.

"I want you to do better than I did, son," said Mr. Bauer, as he gave Gordon a check to help with living expenses.

"You did pretty well, Dad," Gordon said, blurting it out thought-lessly, wondering afterward what he could have meant, since he always thought his father had the worst job in the world, and never imagined himself in similar circumstances, walking the floors trying to persuade people that a Speedy King washer and dryer were the best things a body could own.

The money side of a five to six-year adventure in graduate school was the real problem for Gordon. He was offered a fellowship but living in New York was more expensive than he had imagined. He had some savings, a thousand-dollar scholarship from the Bellflower Chamber of Commerce, a student loan, and his father's gift which could get him through the first year, but the rest was up to chance. When he moved to Manhattan he was appalled in very short order by how much things cost in the city of outstretched hands. His minuscule, dark flat was the best he could find on the Upper West

Side, although being just four blocks south of 125th Street, it was almost in Harlem. He knew his parents would be horrified if he had told them that. "Very near the university and quite lively," is how he described it to them.

Jane Freymiller had not been pleased at all with his leaving, and said she wasn't likely to wait for him. In their last night together she had maliciously refused him even a farewell touch of her breasts. He shrugged it off, however, having heard stories of the women of New York. They were available, eager, and uninhibited. He would be one of the few unmarried heterosexual men there, too, he postulated. Sadly, this was all untrue, or at least untrue to his ability to utilize it. Shyness and the overwhelming workload had conspired thus far against him having any dates, much less amours. He had, alas, spent the first year of graduate school in dismal and unremitting celibacy. There were a few women he eyed, but their eyes were elsewhere: on work, on other men, on other women. Gordon felt as if several million females were assiduously ignoring him.

He had crammed from the beginning of his studies, having been nearly frightened to death the first day on campus as he stood in front of the Butler Library. Reading the names "Plato*Aristotle*Demosthenes" inscribed on the frieze had drained him of all his self-confidence. He was bright by Loyola standards, but his competition there was the progeny of middle-class Irish civil servants and German insurance agents. Now his classmates were blue-eyed prep school boys who had done classics since Phillips Exeter, and olive-skinned Jewish maidens from Long Island with braces and grating accents who had been to schools like Yale and Mt. Holyoke.

But Gordon summoned up his Midwestern determination and

decided he was no less favored by nature to understand iambic pentameter or the aorist tense. He finished his first year with As and Bs in courses like classical philology, Latin poets, and Greek tragedy, as well as an infuriating seminar on Herodotus with the vainglorious Dr. Michael Fontana, Stenley Professor of Greek and Chairman of the Classics Department.

Fontana conducted the entire course in a tone that wandered between ridicule and ennui. Gordon found his professor's comments often going beyond an attack on Herodotus to an assault on Gordon himself because he had naively expressed a love for the Greek historian on the first day of class.

"Herodotus is hardly a historian," Fontana said. "A fabulist, an entertainer, a flat-out liar, perhaps, but not a historian."

He glowered at Gordon intermittently during lectures, as if to question his continued presence in the course. When Gordon went to him to discuss possible dissertation topics relating to Herodotus, Fontana registered a look of disbelief.

"'I only teach this course since we have to offer it every third year. No one else in the department wants to take it, so I assign it to myself out of obligation," he sighed, "as well as a belief that you all would be better off with my dismissiveness than someone else's foolish praise of him."

Gordon skulked off defeated when Fontana concluded by saying he would have grave doubts about any student's intellectual seriousness who wanted to do a doctoral dissertation on Herodotus.

"That means me," Gordon lamented to himself, sure that having antagonized the chairman of his department, he had put the crown of thorns onto the already undistinguished beginnings of an academic career.

If he vaguely felt joie de vivre had slipped through his grasp in the first year, he assured himself that there would be life after a doctorate, although he fretted that by then he wouldn't know life if it jumped up and bit him on the hindquarters. Sometimes he would look out his window at pigeons on the ledge and think they were better off than he was: at least they didn't know they were pigeons.

His fellowship work for the first semester consisted of proofreading all the department's written material; course guides, dissertation regulations, and the like for a revised edition. His Herculean labors on that project were rewarded in the spring with a better opportunity. He became a part-time curatorial assistant at Columbia's Penniman Collection of Classical Antiquities, a rumbling old wing of Mandeville Hall, home of the classics department. There he happily spent nine hours a week helping to catalogue odd fragments of pottery and broken tablets which had been discovered in a boiler room.

This June afternoon, as Gordon continued to walk down Amsterdam Avenue, he considered the unusual circumstances of the lecture he would attend. Dr. Fontana was presenting what he termed "a tour de force of scholarship" on a Greek amphora that had long been in Columbia's possession and had resided until recently in a glass case in the Penniman's small viewing room. It was now the subject of immense controversy and art world interest because Fontana had announced a month before that he could establish beyond any reasonable doubt that it was an artifact whose close inspection would show the connection to black Africa which had long been speculated to have influenced, perhaps even caused Hellenic culture. Found in 1911 in a long-lost tomb in Halicarnassus, once a Greek colony and now in Western Turkey, by a Columbia graduate and amateur archaeologist, the vase was long considered typical of its period and style. Fontana, however, maintained that close scholarly inspection revealed distinct markings and other attributes not found in other vases.

"Further research into art technique, symbolism, ceramic material, pictographic aspects, subtle semiotic clues, and cultural tie-ins establishes a clear similarity to earlier art and artifacts from Egypt and Sudan," he had said pompously at a news conference back in May. He dubbed what was known as Vase 97.156 "The Black Amphora of Halicarnassus," and a storm of controversy immediately ensued culminating in a barrage of letters to *The New York Times*. Classicists debunked the claim as another example of campus political correctness and a rejection of the paramount nature of Western civilization, while their opponents hailed it as a breakthrough for multiculturalism and a truer history of the ancient world.

The lecture had been arranged by Professor William Longstreet, Professor of Classics and Curator of the Penniman Collection. An ardent traditionalist, he doubted Fontana "from the get-go," but insisted that the theory was worth a hearing. Longstreet was sixty-five and had inherited the Penniman appointment as a consolation prize when he stopped being department chair, something he attributed to a covert coup d'etat that had been orchestrated by Fontana.

"He made it all sound as if I were being elevated when in fact I was demoted," Longstreet laughed when he explained it to Gordon.

When he laughed too hard, however, he broke into a dry cough that escalated to the point of near breathlessness, which Gordon sometimes feared to be approaching imminent spontaneous asphyxiation.

As the sun descended below the roof line of the buildings on the west side of Amsterdam, he crossed 120th Street and looked right, examining the rising tower of Riverside Church and thinking of the park beyond, which was his one isle of beauty to embrace in the bleak city. Beauty was on his mind for another reason this evening; one of the journalists who would be in attendance was a woman he had met at the press conference.

"Zera Alpert," he had said a hundred times to himself in the past few weeks, conferring on such a straightforwardly eccentric name a projected loveliness of language, as if it were on a par with "Lauren de Vere", "Isabella Casteneda", or even "Annapaola Antonuccio", all names of imaginary women he had more or less invented in his lengthy adolescence as likely mates for himself.

But Zera Alpert had nothing to do with those others; she wore no flowing gowns, hadn't long, straight hair, and showed no tendency to comport herself as a medieval princess. She was blunt-spoken and even profane, bold and abrupt, but attractive in a way Gordon had never found to be. With a shock of brown, curly hair, a prominent but handsome nose, and full, sensuous lips, she was in a word, bewitching, and had in the short time he watched and listened to her question Fontana, left Gordon smitten. Witty, vivacious, and perceptive, she worked for *The Twelfth Street Liberator,* a sort of leftist tabloid with investigative reporting, odd personal ads, and ink that ran off in your hands on a summer day.

Despite his nearly fatal case of reticence, he was determined tonight to ask Zera out. None but the brave, he kept telling himself, deserved the fair.

When Gordon entered the Columbia campus at 116th Street, he made straight for the lecture hall, a small amphitheater in the Penniman beneath the rotunda. A safe containing the now famous amphora had been wheeled out onto the lecture stage and would be opened in the usual Fontana way, Gordon thought: with drama and puffery. A university security guard stood at one side in what Gordon thought was a piece of showmanship worthy of Barnum. For the month before the event, Fontana's office had created a blizzard of press releases touting the triumph of Afrocentrism. The letters to the *Times* had continued unabated in support of or in opposition to Fontana's thesis. The anticipation of the lecture had created a security problem as supporters and opponents had come to demonstrate. When Gordon approached the front door of Mandeville Hall, he saw picketers with signs which read: "The Greeks Were European," countered by another group with a banner saying: "Homer Go Home". Taunts were thrown back and forth as Columbia security officers and a detail of New York City police kept them apart.

The classicists, people of both sexes with horn-rimmed glasses and bad haircuts, held up a huge photo of the Parthenon and shouted: "Deconstruct This," while the Afrocentrists, most of whom were Caucasian, wore traditional tribal dress and banged on drums while reciting lines of the Odyssey with a war-like tone.

"Eim Odysseus, Laertea-des," a man in a flowing robe began, followed by the chanting of a crowd of people standing behind him.

Inside the building, Gordon saw some of the classics faculty and other graduate students. Once again, he had chosen the wrong wardrobe, as everyone else was informal while he had the stuffed, rigid look of an Illinois storm door salesman.

Gordon ducked into the men's room to comb his hair. His stomach was grumbling sourly now and he took a deep breath. He straightened his tie, which in better light didn't match the suit. His look was neither businesslike nor fashionable, just nerdy. He was so bland looking that he had been selected to be photographed for the Columbia admissions homepage, he suspected to assure potential students that Midwesterners were welcome. He was photographed in a heavy cardigan sweater (although the library was nearly 85 degrees)), sitting at a carrel with the caption, "Mr. Gordon Bauer, a graduate student in classics, studying a medieval Latin manuscript."

In the lobby, people milled about a table where the usual university fare was presented. There were pasty finger sandwiches and forlorn fruit plates, while two undergraduates, a man and a woman each with a ponytail, served jug Chablis in little plastic cups. Gordon took one of the cups and drank it down, followed by a second and then a third in the hope it would calm his nerves. He had only been drunk once in his life, as a freshman at Loyola. Since then he had mostly avoided alcohol in the belief he had a low tolerance for it, but tonight he felt emancipated from his fear. He was older now, a man, he told himself. He would flush away his anxieties about asking Zera out with the oldest of remedies: courage from a bottle. He had a fourth, and since the vessels were small, a fifth. He was buoyant and in control. He felt ebullient, debonair, and irresistible. After a sixth glass, luminous rays of revelation came over him as he weaved through the bodies in the lobby and felt transfigured in the fluorescent light that fell on him. He saw it all now; he was a confident and assertive alpha dog ready to stake his claim. His feet shuffled but his thoughts raced. As people started going inside the lecture hall to take seats, Gordon saw Dr. Fontana shaking hands with several reporters who had been dispatched to cover the latest battle in the culture wars. A Mephistophelean leer pierced through his well-groomed whiskers, and he charmed his circle with wit.

Gordon began searching for a seat and looking for Zera at the same time. The hall was filling rapidly while photographers and sound technicians finished setting up their equipment in the aisles and near the stage. It was then that Gordon saw Zera and one lone seat next to her in the second row. He scurried for it before anyone else could get there, and as he sat next to her, he stared intently while waiting for her to notice him, but the moment turned into a full minute, so unobtrusive was his presence. He gawked at her shapely figure visible through a sheer silk green and yellow pantsuit while she typed something into the tablet she had on her lap. Her hennaed hair changed color in the light, going from dark brown to burnished auburn. She wore one earring of plain gold, while the other was a ceramic parrot from which a feather dangled as a tail, touching her neck as it batted back and forth with the up and down movements of her head. She was arrestingly beautiful, and Gordon decided she looked unbearably intelligent, certainly more intelligent than his toaster, which had been his only companion across the breakfast table for the last ten months. He needed a woman, he decided, and more perilously, he needed this woman.

"Hello again," Gordon said to her, leaning his head forward almost into her line of sight.

She looked at him blankly, her earring shaking and the feather bobbing.

"Gordon Bauer; I met you at the press conference last month?" he said, feeling his awkwardness washing over him and his face growing redder as he waited for some sign of recognition from her. His stomach gurgled as the silence rushed in his ears.

"Oh sure," she said without smiling, looking back at her tablet and resuming her pecking.

"Do you have an angle to your story yet?" he asked.

She glared at him. "I think the 'angle' as you call it is self-explanatory. The notion that Western culture rules the roost is going to get a rude shaking if it's proven black people were in there at the beginning to jump-start it. I had Dr. Fontana for a humanities class when I was at Barnard, and he changed the way I think about many things. He is a visionary."

Gordon couldn't think of anything to say but continued to be mesmerized by her earrings and her lips. His head felt light and the objects in the room began swimming and moving.

Dr. Fontana strode down the aisle and took the podium exactly at five o'clock. He was tall, had dark hair so neatly parted that Gordon thought it included a hairpiece, and a dark mustache and goatee that seemed either scholarly or satanic depending on the room lighting. He gestured to the crowd and spread his papers out. He looked annoyed that the moderator's chair was empty. Professor Longstreet was not in his place, and so Fontana began without an introduction.

"My remarks here will not be extended. A more detailed presentation will be available in the latest edition of *Classical Journal* which comes out tomorrow. Today we are celebrating a breakthrough in the field."

He began outlining the theory of African origins of Greek culture, lambasting traditional classicists, praising Afrocentrists, and making all manner of intemperate remarks about "dead white males" who were mistakenly thought to be the originators of Western civilization. Saying Martin Bernal's *Black Athena* had not taken the theory far enough, Fontana proclaimed, "Africa is where it all started, and we must stand today and make a vast apology to that culture."

The only black professor there was Dr. Calvin Harwell from

the history department, but instead of endorsing what he heard, he shook his head from side to side in quiet but exasperated disagreement. Gordon had solicited his opinion when Fontana's lecture was announced.

Harwell had said, "There is enough to boast about in African civilization without making it up. The ancient Kingdom of Kush, for example, or the Songhai Empire which was literate nine hundred years ago. Art, music, commerce…I don't have to overturn a statue of Sophocles for self-esteem."

Gordon wondered if Fontana's gift for self-promotion was the real way to get ahead in academic life. Fontana was known to be angling for the Arthur Fleming University Professorship, a chair endowed heavily by a family of near epic misfortune. The Fleming's son Artie had been an undergraduate at the time of the great upheavals of 1968 and had died that revolutionary spring, not from police beatings or trampling by a mob, but rather from falling down an elevator shaft, stark naked, while under the spell of a bad batch of LSD. Columbia University, with a battery of lawyers, had persuaded the Flemings, pere et mere, that Artie's name would best be remembered by a gift, not a messy trial with sordid news stories.

Gordon listened as Fontana went on and on about the vase in his diatribe against traditional classical studies, but kept darting glances at Zera, who seemed transfixed by Fontana. As Gordon studied Fontana's looks, he decided the arching eyebrows and facial hair made him look like a perfect satyr. He thought of the professor having sex with Zera the young undergraduate, and imagined them having every kind of sex, for during the Herodotus seminar there always seemed time for Fontana to digress on the erotic oddities of the ancient world. But Fontana's words that evening grew less comprehensible to Gordon. He felt dizzy and unbalanced, as if standing on a ship's deck in a bad gale. He wanted to lean toward Zera and say something brilliant, but nothing whatsoever, clever or stupid, came to mind. His brain was a huge, blank slate, a hayrick of limp hay, a puddle of incoherence. He was, he realized, sadly, irreparably, and monumentally drunk.

It was then that Gordon's stomach made churning warnings to him that he was not going to escape being sick. As Fontana moved to his peroration and announced that the vault door would be swung open to reveal the amphora, Gordon got up and made for the aisle. His hands were clammy and his mouth dry. He wobbled past the security guard and out of the building, gasping for fresh air. Things were very blurry then, and the heads of the people moving across the campus walkways seemed gray-green in the evening twilight. He thought to himself before sickness overtook him that they looked like heads of broccoli. Gordon knew then that "too much to drink" for him meant anything after the first glass.

Then rebellion of his stomach was now complete, nausea churning his insides, and he leaned over and vomited, aware at the last moment that his necktie would not be a survivor. He lurched forward onto the ground, dizzy and shaking. He crawled on all fours to a pathetic little tree sprouting in the middle of asphalt, leaning back against it in agony. A few minutes later he threw up again, painfully and violently. He huffed in air and tried to get to his feet, but almost immediately fell down again. He spat out a vile taste in his mouth, and while still hunched over vomited yet again, retching and grunting on his hands and knees. That last regurgitation emptied him, so he thought, of whatever remained of the finger sandwiches, the wine, the chicken curry, his brains, and yea, his very soul. He crawled back to the tree, sat and rested his head, and fell asleep, only to be awakened sometime later by the sound of a police siren.

There was noise from Mandeville Hall by then, and he saw the blue flash of police lights from the Broadway entrance and several squad cars pulling in along College Walk and driving toward the Penniman. The police got out and ran inside. An ambulance and more campus police were on the scene, and Gordon sat there trying to put his thoughts together as he watched the colors and shapes moving and running in all directions. People milled about, and once again he thought he would be sick, but it was only dry heaves at this point and his barfing and groaning drew the attention of those standing nearby. When he looked up and focused his eyes, the first face he saw was connected to a dangling earring and he heard Zera Alpert's voice speaking to him.

"Are you all right?"

Gordon tried to answer her, sure he looked like some pathetic dog.

"You shouldn't drink this way if you can't handle it," she said disapprovingly. "Do you want me to call for help?"

He reached for his handkerchief to wipe his mouth, trying at the same time to explain that something he ate had made him sick, that he certainly wasn't drunk.

"Shrur-tanly not dunk," he slurred.

"I'd call you a cab but I've got a story breaking," she said, and Gordon looked at her quizzically.

"Wuh story?" he said with a burp.

"The amphora was gone when they opened the safe door," she said, "and then they found Professor Longstreet in his office dead."

"Dread?" Gordon asked.

"No, dead; it looks like someone killed him and popped the vase."

She left him to go back to the circle of reporters being briefed by a detective. Gordon tried to compose his thoughts and process that the vase was stolen and the curator gone for the long boat ride across the Styx with Charon the ferryman. It made no sense, but neither did the two policemen coming toward him with the security officer who had been by the door when Gordon bolted the lecture hall.

"There, he's the one," the security man said to the police, pointing a finger at Gordon like an accusatory sausage, wagging meaty and plump in the air as it called down this malediction upon him.

II

"I can't be dead; I have tenure"

GORDON GOT TO HIS FEET, and the policemen took him by the arms and walked him to the entrance of Mandeville Hall. There a portly man in a cheap, wrinkled suit with an unlit cigar hanging from his mouth directed Gordon to sit on a stone bench outside the double doors.

"I'm Detective Sabatini, and I want to ask you some questions," he began, sounding skeptical even before Gordon had a chance to speak.

"Name?"

"Gordon Bauer."

"Address?"

"431 West 121st Street, Apartment 4-B."

"Do you have some ID?"

Gordon pulled out his wallet and handed Sabatini his driver's license.

"Says here you live in Chicago, Illinois."

Gordon scratched his nose and looked for his Columbia student ID.

"I did live in Chicago before I came here," he said, and gave the detective another card.

"This says you can borrow books from the Bellflower, Illinois Public Library."

"Sorry," Gordon answered, realizing he hadn't found the Columbia card. After fishing out a Mobil gas card, a Sears's credit card, a bank ATM card, and a membership in the German-American Cultural Society, he found the Columbia ID. He smiled with idiotic pride when he held it out to Sabatini.

The detective patiently recorded all the information, questioning him for twenty minutes about the department, his job, and what he knew of the now-missing amphora.

"All right, you wait here," he said before going off to interview several more people, including Professor Fontana whom Gordon saw standing in the vestibule.

A uniformed policeman remained with Gordon, who by now was alert enough to observe what was happening, although not yet sober enough to fully comprehend it. Zera Alpert came back with her notebook and looked at Gordon with a kind of pathetic disdain. His hair was tousled and damp, his face pale, and he had grass stains on the knees of his pants while his shoes and trouser cuffs bore the marks of his gastric upheavals.

"This is getting deep," she said. "Longstreet was found dead in his office with his wallet and watch missing, and the police don't know if it's connected with the stolen amphora."

Gordon was trying to replace all his cards in the plastic pockets of his billfold as Zera watched. He tucked one in, then another, and realizing it was upside down, reversed it, aware this little exercise was dodging matters of graver importance.

"Do they think you know anything about this?" she asked bluntly.

It was then that it dawned on him through the clouds of his obliviousness that he could be in serious trouble. He tried to speak, but only a burp came forth from his open mouth,

"Would you like me to get you some soda?" she said.

"Yes, please," he answered, and she went inside the building to a vending machine and bought two cans of ginger ale. The balmy June breeze touched Gordon's face as she walked back to where he was, and he felt as if he were being ministered to by the reincarnation of Florence Nightingale herself.

The lights of Mandeville Hall were all on now as the police and university security conducted a room-by-room search of the building. Gordon looked up at the windows and saw figures moving on the staircase and in the offices and classrooms. A black SUV with panels instead of windows pulled into the walkway by the building. Several men drew a gurney out of the back and unfolded it, taking it in the direction of Professor Longstreet's office. A while later they came back down with the gurney, a sealed black plastic bag the size of a man strapped to it. They put it into the back of the vehicle, the legs and wheels snapping up as it was pushed forward. The men closed the doors and got into the wagon. Gordon saw a seal painted on the door which said, "Office of the Medical Examiner". A hush fell over the bystanders as the wagon drove away, everyone having watched enough police dramas to know what was happening. An emptiness came over Gordon, and he suddenly felt exhausted. The classicists who had been demonstrating stood in one corner of the grassy patch by Mandeville, their signs laid flat on the ground. The Africanists likewise, from a position on the opposite side, put down their drums and banners as they waited their turn to be interrogated. Both sides looked at each other like football players on opposite teams, eager to mix it up and begin blocking and tackling again, but who found their game called to a halt by the referee's whistle when an infraction demanding a penalty had been incurred. A few on either side, Gordon thought, might be grasping the fact that onto arcane ideological debate, the shadow of real life sometimes fell.

The detectives continued taking statements from people, and finally at ten o'clock everyone was told they were free to go.

"But we'll be talking with you again on this; don't leave town without calling me," Sabatini said, and handed Gordon his card.

"Are you all right to get home alone?" Zera asked Gordon.

"I guess," he said, his stomach and head aching.

"Why don't you take a cab?" she said.

"It's just a few streets up Amsterdam; I can make it on my own."

"I'm dubious," she said, this time with almost a smile. "Why don't I go with you?"

He burped again, then sighed, unable to disagree very strenuously.

"Come on," she said, and steered him by the elbow toward Amsterdam Avenue. "I need to get more information on this story. This could be my big break; if you help me, I'll help you, since the police don't seem to have ruled you out as a suspect. What do you say?"

"Sure," he answered reflexively, feeling afterward that he had been dealt the New York con, the quick sell, the sleight of hand.

When they reached Gordon's apartment, it was apparent she was inviting herself upstairs. They went to his flat, trudging step by step to the fourth floor. He felt as if he had been in a fight and had not only lost, but had been used to mop the ring. On the third-floor landing a group of darker-skinned young men were standing at an open door. One nodded to Gordon. They seemed to be concluding a meeting, and when Gordon looked inside, he saw a flag with two red stripes on a field of green and a crescent moon over a snow-capped mountain. A sign under the flag with both English and Arabic letters read "The Popular Front for A Free Ululistan".

"You like maybe to read some literature?" one of them said, handing a pamphlet to Gordon while smiling at Zera.

"Thanks," he said, accepting it with one of his hands.

"Our country is very small, but very much in suffering," the man called up to Gordon as he ascended the next flight of stairs. "We need support to overthrow the despot and have democracy and rights."

Gordon ruminated on the words, wondering why anyone who lived for even one day in the most obnoxiously and flatulently democratic city in the world, where everyone had rights but was still miserable, would want to replicate such a situation in his own homeland. On the fourth-floor landing Gordon fumbled for the several keys and coaxed the door into opening. Once they were inside, he flipped off his shoes and poured some water into a glass, adding two Alka Seltzer tablets.

"Why don't you get out of those clothes," she said, gesturing him into the tiny bedroom with a wave of her hand. He wished she had been saying them in some erotic way, but clearly she wasn't. The stains from his vomiting were revolting, and she turned away to avoid looking at them any longer.

Gordon retreated to the room and closed the door, then and

tossed off his jacket, pants, shirt and underwear and got into pajamas, blue cotton ones from Macy's with little sailboats and nautical flags on them. He came back into the front room and collapsed into the overstuffed seat, while Zera sat across from him in a wooden chair and positioned her notebook on her knee.

"Now what makes this vase so valuable; that it is ancient and rare, or that it is the center of this controversy?"

Gordon thought for a moment, struggling to line up nouns with verbs, separate presumptions from conclusions, and distinguish facts from mere opinions.

"Well the vase is valuable by itself, I understand from Professor Longstreet, based on being in excellent condition undisturbed in a sealed tomb for centuries."

"And the African connection?" she said, badgering like a cross-examining attorney. "Do you think someone stole it because of Fontana's claims about it?"

"Hard to say; I suppose anything famous or notorious has increased value."

Gordon was pleased with his bluff savvy, his voice of authority even with a pounding headache.

"But this would make it harder to fence," she added triumphantly, "unless you dealt with a shady dealer, or it was stolen to order by someone who wanted it specifically."

"Yes, I suppose," Gordon said, although stolen artwork was not a subject he had any familiarity with before that night.

She crossed her legs back and forth as she sat in front of him, occasionally flipping her hair to one side. He was falling deeper and deeper into absorption with every gesture or facial expression she made.

"Tell me about Professor Longstreet," she said.

"He was a gentleman, a real scholar," Gordon began.

"A bookish don, a squirrel hoarding intellectual tidbits?"

Gordon took offense at her characterization, and it was apparent to her as she began a retreat.

"I only meant in the sense of being a typical academic; one who studies the world rather than inhabits it," she said.

"I think he had an enviable life," Gordon replied, but unsure now whether he really meant it. Long hours spent hunting down etymologies and reading arcane journal articles on literary theory suddenly seemed less purposeful than when he had started graduate school. He loved the Latin and Greek authors and the ancient world they wrote about, but modern-day glosses with titles such as "The Hermeneutics of Suspicion in Oedipus Rex", and "The Rhetoric of Alterity" had put him in a state of doubt by the spring semester.

There was a pause as Zera punched something into her tablet and then resumed her questions.

"Can you imagine any reason someone would want to kill Longstreet?"

"None," Gordon said emphatically.

"Someone who had a grudge or rivalry?"

Gordon shook his head from side to side, but when he did it began to hurt again.

"Did he ever say anything that suggested he had premonitions of dying?"

"No, just the opposite. He seemed to relish being a professor, and that he would go on this way until a very old age."

Zera shrugged. "No one ever thinks he is the one who will die, that the honors and titles will somehow grant longevity if not immortality." She let out a breath of air and fumbled in her purse for a cigarette. Looking at his pained expression, she put the package back. "I'm sorry; I'm sure the last thing you want to smell right now is smoke."

"I don't mind," he said in a total lie.

"It's all right. I'm trying to quit."

Zera got up from where she sat and paced the room for a minute, mumbling to herself. "All right. We have a professor with a theory, another professor with an unanticipated date with the grim reaper, a missing Greek vase, and no suspects except a graduate student who looks like hell."

She smiled at him and he smiled back, laughing a bit although his stomach muscles hurt.

"So Longstreet is your hero; dry, detached, and cerebral. What do you think of Fontana?"

"That he's egotistical and self-promoting."

"Fontana is a man with his feet planted in life; perhaps he wants to rise in the world because he believes he has abilities others don't," Zera said. "What you call self-promoting is just the wish to be heard."

"I suppose you could say that," Gordon replied. "But he's what most people would call a phony."

"Well I thought he was a dynamic teacher," she said, emphasizing "dynamic".

Then Gordon, in a burst of directness unthinkable before he had come to New York said, "You were lovers, then?"

Zera put on a look of haughty coolness. "No, we weren't, but that tells me how your mind works."

"I'm sorry," he said, offering an apology to someone he barely knew but had managed to insult.

Zera was moved from glacial to empathetic and said, "It's all right. Fontana had a reputation as a flirtatious charmer, so I suspect you assumed I was one of his conquests. I wasn't. I just thought he was a good teacher."

Gordon reached for a tissue and blew his nose. He felt wretched and urgently wanted to lie down. He yawned and Zera looked at her watch. It was now almost midnight.

"A few more questions and I'll go," she said. "First; is there someone else in the department who would steal the vase?"

Gordon said no, but realized he knew no more about anyone else's motivation than he did about particle accelerators.

"When was the amphora last on public view?"

Gordon rubbed his forehead for a moment. "The week you came to interview Fontana it was in its case at the Penniman, and it remained there until a week ago when Fontana, Longstreet, a security guard, and I moved it from the locked display case to the safe that was in Longstreet's office."

"Who closed the safe?"

"Professor Longstreet closed the door and spun the dial."

"Did he pull the handle to see if it was locked?"

"Yes," Gordon answered.

"And who had the combination?"

"Professor Longstreet alone; he was to write it down and give it to Fontana in a sealed envelope. The security department would wheel the safe from Longstreet's office to the lecture hall before the speech. Fontana would open the envelope in front of the audience, put in the combination, and open the door at the end of his comments."

"And that is exactly what happened," Zera said. "Shortly after you left Fontana finished his remarks and then opened the safe."

"To find …?" Gordon asked.

"Nada, niente, zilch, bupkis," she said, reaching again for her cigarettes and then stopped herself.

Gordon shrugged, unable to conceive how the amphora had disappeared from the safe.

"Where was Longstreet?"

"They found his body down behind his desk; security apparently never saw him when they came to move the safe out to the lecture hall at about four o'clock. The police found him later in their search of the building," Zera said. "If Longstreet didn't take the amphora because he was already dead, it was somehow removed before the safe was brought to the lecture hall, but how, when, and by whom?"

"How about some common thief who forced Professor Longstreet to open the safe sometime in the afternoon while it was still in his office?"

"Possible, I suppose, but why didn't Longstreet call the police then?"

"Because they had already killed him?" Gordon suggested.

"Possible that as well," Zera said, "Although I overheard one detective say there were no visible wounds on the body."

"Maybe someone affiliated with the classics department who knew the amphora was valuable."

"Like you," Zera said playfully.

"I didn't have the combination," Gordon protested.

"Maybe Longstreet wrote it down somewhere, or you watched him open it. He was old, perhaps just not paying attention."

"I still think it was a street criminal," Gordon said. "It is worth a tidy sum of money."

" 'Tidy sum'? Where did you learn to talk that way; 1930s movies?"

Gordon blushed. "Illinois" he said softly.

She frowned and said, "I think this crime is ideological. I believe when the sun sets on this one, it will be one or more people from the neo-conservative racist element who took this because they feared it would spike their Eurocentric theories once and for all. I am sure of it. It is an intellectual crime both in motive and execution!"

She tapped her tablet to exit the document and close the application, and Gordon rose from his chair to open the door for her. He felt as if he were going to be sick again and raced to the bathroom. He got into his knees and gagged, but it was more dry heaves at this point.

"If you don't mind my saying so, maybe you aren't cut out for the drinking life," she shouted from the doorway.

He came back to the room and said, "It was a bad curry."

"Whatever," she said. "If you think of anything by morning, call me. I'll probably be up all night writing this."

She handed him her card, and he looked at it through bleary eyes.

"You don't believe I had anything to do with this, do you? Intellectual crime or any other kind."

She looked at him for a moment and answered, "I don't think you have a criminal manner."

She said good night to him, and he listened to her footsteps down the stairwell. The true meaning of what she said occurred to him. "She meant you aren't man enough to do anything, much less pull off a crime," he said to himself.

He reflected through his haze that perhaps all his relationships with women had been colored by a certain lack of assertiveness, an unwillingness to take the lead. He had been brought up in a genteel way and, being a sensitive young man, had always put politeness first and never sought to dominate or command a woman. He respected women and believed in equality, and yet he lately began to feel as if the net result of his willingness to always defer to someone else, man or woman, was not politeness or respect for others, but some huge feeling of inadequacy which caused him to surrender before a battle had even begun. Was being too nice really not nice at all, but craven?

He remembered the trip he had taken in the summer before senior year at Loyola. The classics majors joined students from other Jesuit colleges on a three-week tour of Italy and Greece to inspect ruins, read inscriptions, and visit museums. The days were filled with learning, but evenings were more socializing at little cafes and bars. One of the girls, Caitlin Ryan from Georgetown, was extroverted and sophisticated, quite unlike most of the others who were as bookish and shy as Gordon. He found her quite attractive, although he was dating Jane who was back in Chicago waitressing for the summer on a day cruise boat on Lake Michigan. But seeing no sin in harmless flirtation, he took every opportunity to sit next to her, and in so doing became more and more aflame with desire. He felt loyalty to Jane, but thought perhaps marrying the first woman he slept with was something which could lead to illicit temptations later. Better if he were to have a fling, to do it before settling down, and Jane had not been a virgin anyway when he met her, something he thought was a good thing at the time, in that it allowed for at least one person in the equation to know what to do.

One evening he was with Caitlin and some others at a small restaurant in Athens. She was laughing, telling stories, and frequently grabbing his arm for emphasis on some point. She had half a bottle of wine and Gordon felt this night would be his opportunity. Just then three young men, athletes from USC, who had been touring Europe heard Caitlin's English and came over.

"Sit with us, grab some chairs," Caitlin said to them, and before the next round of drinks was consumed, Gordon found himself on the periphery of the conversation. The three men had quickly coupled with Caitlin and two other women from his group, and Gordon was the seventh wheel, slinking out the door to go back to the hotel without saying goodnight as no one seemed very interested in his leave-taking. Gordon knew six other people who would be having sex that night as he lay in his bed reading a paperback copy of Walter Leaf's translation of the *Iliad*. He knew of Walter Leaf, a true Renaissance man, a London banker with training in classics who combined a businessman's life with literary studies, doing translations from Greek, Latin, Persian, and Arabic. He had kept his two lives so separate that when he died, two groups of people came to his funeral: his classics friends from Trinity College, Cambridge, and men of commerce from the City. Both groups when they began interacting, it was said, were convinced they were at the funeral of the wrong Walter Leaf. Lacking the verve to make his way in the world, Gordon had chosen academic life by default. Perhaps, he thought now, it wasn't a choice but rather an abdication.

Weary now from his long evening, he wandered to the couch and thought about his relationship with Jane. She seemed as content as he was with their being together, and as undergraduates, they never raised the subject of marriage except in a general way. After graduation when he taught high school, she took a position as a receptionist in a child welfare agency to see if she liked that world well enough to pursue graduate study in social work. In November of that year they went to Bellflower because his sister was getting married. Gordon's family liked Jane because she was pleasant-tempered, pretty in a German sort of way, and his mother thought she was maternal.

At the wedding, Jane wanted to dance, but Gordon could only do the lame man's two-step to slow music, so Jane and the other women took to the dance floor and shook, slid, and gyrated to the latest tunes done by a loud cover band hired for the occasion. At the after-party Chez Bauer, people stayed as long as their fatigue let them, but by midnight they were all gone. Gordon's parents, brother, and aunt retired, and he went upstairs to brush his teeth. Jane was staying in his sister's room as the honeymoon couple had left for Aruba. Gordon fell asleep but at two A.M. he was awakened when Jane came into his room, pulled off her nightgown, and slipped into Gordon's bed.

"Jane," he said.

"They're all asleep," she whispered, "and have had enough alcohol to keep an elephant down until morning."

"My parents might hear us."

"Not unless one of us starts screaming."

Her body was warm as she began to pull his pajamas off.

"Jane, you should go back to your room; we'll be by ourselves in Chicago tomorrow night."

She frowned. "You're no fun."

"They would think less of you if they knew."

"Cluck, bruck-cluck," she said, making chicken noises as she got up, put her nightgown back on and left his room.

Nothing more was said of it, and at Christmas Gordon went with Jane to see her parents in Eau Claire. They went to midnight mass, had dinner on Christmas, and Gordon left the next day to go to Bellflower. He was back in Chicago for New Year's Eve, and at midnight she puckered up for a kiss but seemed to be waiting for something else after he had kissed her. On New Year's Day she was not in a good mood and barely spoke when they had brunch with some of her friends. Gordon called his sister that night and told her about Jane.

"She was expecting you to propose, nitwit," his sister said.

"But I haven't a job that pays enough to live on, and won't for a while if I go to graduate school; why would she expect me to propose?"

"Because you've gone out with her for four years. People usually take the next step by then."

"Doesn't sound practical to me," Gordon demurred.

"Aaagh; I can't stand it!" his sister groaned. "Of course, it's not practical. Making love and making babies, buying a house and having mortgage payments for thirty years; none of that is practical. Love is not practical, Gordon! Whoever told you it was?"

Gordon sulked for a long time; what his sister said was probably true, but he wasn't ready to accept all that then. He felt he couldn't just yet settle into a life of 'till death do we part.

"Death? I haven't lived yet!" he exclaimed, but didn't have the courage to say that to Jane.

They drifted on as they both applied to graduate school, Jane saying there was no reason he couldn't go to Chicago or Northwestern and stay with her. His acceptance at Columbia was the beginning of the end, and he realized he had already made the choice of becoming unglued from her.

He was weary now but not ready to go to sleep until he knew he would not get sick again. Turning on the television, he watched the all-night local news channel for the story of the theft. The stock market had dropped three hundred points, the talking head began in a litany of the day's occurrences. A warlord had massacred a thousand people in Africa while famine gripped the country; two fires and a murder took place in Manhattan; a water main had ruptured on Eighth Avenue; a homeless man had been set on fire; a seeing eye dog was missing; a movie star was seeking her fifth divorce to remarry her third husband; a glass jar of fruit exploded and injured a child in Brooklyn and the mother already had an attorney; a PATH train to Hoboken had gotten stuck in the tunnel during rush hour; a plane had blown a tire while landing at LaGuardia; a phone scam soliciting money for refugees it never helped was uncovered; Gordon's favorite candy bar from childhood, Yum-Yum, was being discontinued because only old people from the Midwest bought them; and the solemn voice of the health beat reporter said new findings showed a possible connection between bladder damage and eating too much rhubarb while taking aspirin. Gordon sat in a half stupor trying to decide if he ever had a headache concurrent with a craving for rhubarb pie, what would be his odds.

"Crime comes to Columbia University," the newscaster finally said, telling of the missing amphora, the death of Longstreet, and the police investigation. They flashed a picture of Professor Longstreet on the screen, and Gordon felt a genuine unhappiness that the one person in the classics department he truly liked was dead.

After the news came sports and weather. It would rain tomorrow, the jovial, rotund meteorologist said, and the female sportscaster with a deep voice and muscular torso announced that the loathed Yankees had beaten his Chicago White Sox 5 to 3.

Gordon flipped off the set, turned out the lights, and stumbled into bed. The green digital numbers of his clock radio said 2:14 A.M. A siren wailed and then faded. There was no music from the flat above his, and as nearly as it could ever be, Manhattan was at rest. He lay there considering his situation; he was broke with no prospects, he had met an entrancing woman whose interest in him seemed limited to his ability to provide information on a criminal case, and he was quite likely to be dragged through a police inquiry. He thought of Professor Longstreet and felt a great sadness pull at him. A dedicated teacher and scholar was in the end noted more for the manner of his dying than the accomplishments of his life. It gave Gordon considerable pause as to whether he wanted such a career. An even greater pause came when the next thought struck him: if he was accused of stealing an ancient treasure, what possible future could he have in the classics?

He knew the field of ancient studies was large enough to accommodate the brilliant and the less brilliant, the conservative and the liberal, the socially awkward, the misfits, geek boys, frigid girls, compulsive grammarians, and haters of modernity, as well as numerous drunkards, sloths, pederasts, fornicators, egotists, poseurs, and buffoons, but not as far as he knew, any kleptomaniacs.

"One can do anything with the classics," he thought, "except get rich by them."

Gordon rolled over and pulled his pillow tightly to his face. When he was a boy, he had a teddy bear named Fred that he told his troubles to, and wished for a moment, even though he was technically an adult, that he had the bear again. He pushed his face further into the pillow and imagined it was Jane Freymiller. The mental nexus between the stuffed animal and his former girlfriend startled him into a recognition that perhaps he subconsciously favored the one because of resembling the other. It was too profoundly disturbing for him to analyze his desires that way, for it implied a certain lack of maturity in him that called for resolution. He thought of Zera before falling asleep; there was a woman no one would confuse with a warm stuffed animal. Zera was a she-wolf, he thought, making the call of the wild from above the timberline, beckoning him to dangerous heights. If he could run fast enough to follow, he told himself, perhaps this would be his long-deferred passage to adulthood.

III

"The night life, it ain't no
good life, but it's my life."

A T EIGHT O'CLOCK THE NEXT morning, Gordon's alarm clock
blared out with relentless insistence. He opened one eye and
thought that his body could be in no worse condition if the sound
had been the angel Gabriel's trumpet signaling him to leave the
tomb and join the general resurrection.

He sat up and immediately felt nauseous. He walked to the
window for some fresh air, but the smell of truck exhaust fumes
greeted him instead. His head ached, his stomach hurt, his throat
was parched, and the muscles of his abdomen reminded him of its
involuntary workout the night before.

"Never again," he muttered, making the drunkard's vow.

He was due to work at the Penniman that morning and thought
of calling in sick, but didn't because it would make him seem suspicious, as well as the fact that his Midwestern sense of duty would
inflict more discomfort on him if he stayed home. Unpleasant ob-
ligations had a righteous significance to Gordon, having always

believed that to endure them made a person better, at least according to his grandmother Irmgard Hasenfus. Oma was never wrong about things like that, he thought.

The sun was fading in anticipation of the clouds and rain that had been forecast. Gordon took a shower beneath the dribbling, leaking attachment hooked up on an arm above the bathtub. He twisted it with one hand, but it stuck, leaving it in a position that sprayed his face with a fine mist while a violent shaft of water in the middle seemed to be boring a hole in his chest. He felt well enough after that to try some toast, but wound up chasing it down with another Alka-Seltzer before leaving the apartment. He wondered if anyone really felt better by taking a drink first thing in the morning, the "hair of the dog".

He walked downstairs slowly, and on the first-floor landing Alma Wyatt was discussing the weather with another tenant, Francis X. Kelley, a frail octogenarian whom Gordon had found out was a retired New York policeman.

"Red sky in morning, sailors take warning," Kelley said.

"When it rains, you'll have pains," Alma replied, nodding her head.

"Morning," Gordon said to both of them, and they repeated the word back.

Gordon thought of how they would spend their days; Alma would watch television, go to the grocery store, and later play cards with two other women who lived on the second floor. Frank Kelley would sit on the steps if the weather was nice and listen to a baseball game on an old transistor radio. He had mourned the death of a spouse many years before and had children he seldom saw.

"My son's a lawyer," Frank would say, "busy all the time."

Gordon thought it was more of an excuse than a boast. At Thanksgiving and Christmas, he had seen a Cadillac Escalade with New Jersey license plates pull up and take the old man to dinner, but they were home before sunset. Another son lived in California, but Gordon had never seen him.

Once when Alma asked Gordon to help her open a stuck window, he saw a picture on the mantelpiece of a black man in an army uniform. A folded flag in a glass case was next to it, and another held a felt board with medals pinned to it.

"My son Eddie. In Iraq," was all she could say when she saw Gordon looking at the picture. "The city was going to put up a plaque at the basketball court on 135th Street where he played when he was a boy, but it never happened."

Alma's husband had left her when Eddie was four and she raised him on her own, surviving somehow as a hospital housekeeper and now on a small pension and social security.

Gordon would run errands for Frank and Alma if they asked, but instead of making him feel good, it only depressed him. New York was hard enough for the young; for the old, it seemed unbearable. He walked down Amsterdam Avenue that morning burdened by all these thoughts, but by the time he arrived at the Penniman Collection he was in a better frame of mind, having thought about Zera for the last three blocks. At eleven o'clock Dr. Fontana showed up to brief the staff of two curatorial assistants, a secretary, and a sleepy-eyed uniformed guard about the death of Professor Longstreet and the missing amphora.

"The police are going to be asking more questions," he said, shooting a look at Gordon. "Professor Longstreet will be greatly missed, but I will be the acting curator of the Penniman, so let's all go about our work and make the best of things, shall we?"

Gordon went to his tiny desk underneath a casement window which was grilled and bolted. He examined the window frame to see if there were any signs of forced entry, getting up from time to time to look at other windows on the basement level. Soon every nook and cranny of the building was being considered by his mind's eye to see where someone could enter. He wasn't sure he could describe a forced entry's exact look, especially given the rattling and decaying condition of many of the doors and windows in the building, but as a judge once said in defining pornography, he would know it when he saw it.

On his break, it occurred to him that one way of finding out what a vase of the Black Amphora's type might be worth would be to ask an art dealer. This might be an indicator as to how sophisticated the thieves were, and if so, be a clue to their identities. He searched the web for dealers in Manhattan and found one which specialized in Greek and Roman antiquities.

"Miltiades Stanopoulos Gallery" their website proclaimed. It was on Madison Avenue and he wrote down the address, intent on going the next day. The following morning he arose feeling better, and he rashly spent cab fare to go to the East Side. On Madison and 81st a shop with an awning and an elegant front window containing pottery, jewelry, and coins on display appeared before him.

He rang the bell, and a man in a dark suit buzzed him in.

"Good morning," the gallery owner said unctuously, eyeing Gordon with some hope that his threadbare outfit might conceal an oil baron's son willing to acquire something at a hugely inflated price.

"I was wondering if you could answer a question for me," Gordon said. "Greek vases of the fourth and fifth century B.C.; what would I have to pay for one now?"

Stanopoulos seemed surprised by the question "That depends on many things," he began, and started to launch into a detailed explanation of all the variables putting a valuation on collectible vases entailed.

"Just roughly, a range," Gordon interjected.

The gallery owner went to the back and produced a book of information on auction sales. He pointed to the long lists, some with pictures, and when Gordon saw one roughly similar to the Penniman amphora, he touched his finger to the page.

"In fine condition, fifty thousand and up, but some might be a quarter of a million depending on the quality of the art and condition and any historical connection or unique attribute," Stanopoulos said, staring at Gordon with expectation as if he might pull out a checkbook.

Gordon looked up at the video cameras recording his presence. "Thanks; that's all I need to know," he said, and made for the door.

"Do you want to buy one?" Stanopoulos called after him.

"No, not now. Perhaps another time."

Outside on Madison the sidewalks were crowded with passersby. It was a fine summer day, and as he walked along a young woman holding some brochures smiled at him.

"Hello," she said.

"Hello," Gordon answered.

"Do you have a moment?"

Thinking that streetwalkers looked more like graduate students these days, he began to demur.

"I'm really late."

"Just a moment; I want to ask you if you could have anything in the world you don't have now, what would it be?"

Gordon stopped in his tracks and thought. "A doctorate" would have been his first answer, but he doubted it was the answer she sought. It didn't matter as she launched into a speech he regretted he hadn't seen coming. Like a left hook in the face, she said, "I'm from the Society for Mental Dynamics, and we believe the most untapped source of human fulfillment is the mind."

He attempted to move past her, but she shoved a pamphlet at him.

"All I ask is that you read this; it gives the secrets to finding happiness that have been locked away since the beginning of time."

"Sorry," he said and began walking double time, turning the corner on 79th in the direction of Fifth Avenue.

The woman matched his strides and thrust a book in front of his face. "The Mind, The World, and You," she said. "It was written by our founder Nehemias Schute; perhaps you've heard of him?"

"Yes, but no," Gordon said, breaking into a near run.

"You can't discover this on your own," she called, standing in the middle of the sidewalk shouting at him.

"Then how did Nehemias do it?" Gordon yelled back at her, turning red in the face. He was embarrassed with what would have been bad manners in Illinois, but which was street survival in New York.

He got back to Fifth Avenue and hailed a taxi to take him to his apartment where, after a bowl of canned chicken soup, he fell into a deep and thoughtless sleep. The ringing of the telephone at three o'clock that afternoon snapped him back to the world of his troubles.

"Hello?" he said.

"Lo," a woman's voice responded, and she waited for him to add to the conversation.

"Hello?" he repeated.

"Hi; is this Gordon Bauer?"

"Yes," he said suspiciously.

"It's Zera," she said, and muttered something to someone in the background. "Have you seen the police report?"

"No," he said glumly.

"Well, it seems Longstreet died of an apparent heart attack, but if it happened while he was being robbed, the robber might face homicide charges since the death would have occurred during the commission of a felony."

"Oh," Gordon said wanly.

"But the vase is still missing and that's what's under investigation. They won't tell me anything more, but can you meet me for dinner tonight so I can go over what I have so far?"

He cheered at her interest but, remembering his stomach's trauma of less than forty-eight hours earlier, said "Maybe something light."

She gave him the address of a natural foods place at West 75th. He agreed and several hours later found himself sitting in a booth with Zera while a waiter with a goatee served them brown rice and miso soup.

"You've had time to ponder this, Gordon. Who do you think stole the thing?"

Gordon unwrapped chopsticks from a plastic package. Zera ate her rice that way, and he did not want to seem less cosmopolitan.

"I think it was your run-of-the-mill street thief or junkie," he offered.

Zera frowned and drew a deep breath before saying, "More than I did last night, I believe it was neo-conservative racist types who jacked the vase since it was about what they feared the most: an African origin for their dear classical civilization."

She twisted in her seat, excited by that notion, as if it not only explained a missing amphora, but all the other things in the world that troubled her.

"I think facts disprove Fontana's theory," Gordon countered, leaning forward with triumph in his voice. He maladroitly picked up a bit of rice with his chopsticks, but it fell into his lap as he moved it in the direction of his mouth.

"What are facts?" she said cynically. "Aren't they just constructs, illusions people hold to prove what is in their interest to believe?"

"Did you read Martin Bernal's *Black Athena*?"

"I know of it, but never read the whole thing."

"Bernal, a scholar with background in languages, wrote a three-volume tome claiming that Greek civilization, which is to say Western, was Afro-Asiatic in origin. He traced what he felt were language origins and other clues to indicate Egyptian and Phoenician civilizations were largely the source of Greek culture and language," Gordon said.

"Right, I remember that part, and he said it was nineteenth-century Europeans who invented the Greek myth, not wanting any African or Semitic bloodlines for the cause."

"But his theories are much disputed," Gordon interjected.

"By people who deny that ancient Egyptians were or could have been black."

"I don't think anyone knows for sure. These are all theories, and I suppose what makes Fontana's claim different is if he can demonstrate convincingly that some of the markings on this amphora are truly African signs or symbols passed down in Greek culture."

"But you are inclined to disbelieve anyway, so why do you care?"

"I actually don't think it is so important where Greek values come from as where they are going. I want to teach Latin and Greek because they are still important. I just think Fontana is a careerist along for the ride and would say anything to be the center of attention."

Zera turned back to her meal and wolfed down a veggie burger tucked in a pita pocket with alfalfa sprouts as the soup and rice had not been enough to sate her hunger. She alternately chewed and expostulated, giving Gordon a forty- minute tour of her political beliefs and philosophy. She was a Marxist at heart, and committed as a journalist to seeking out and denouncing the abuses of power committed by the privileged classes. She had gone to Barnard and idolized the sixties, wishing she could have stormed the barricades at Berkeley, torn up paving stones in Paris, or been tear-gassed at Columbia. Something in her voice intimated that, had she been born in the generation of the "Sixty-Eighters", the revolution might have taken place after all.

Gordon was too intimidated and smitten by her to tell her he thought her views were rubbish. Instead, he grew more mesmerized as she continued. She hated the right, loved egalitarian causes, and wanted to travel to rainforests and barrios to interview revolutionaries. Gordon stared at her in full-blown love. She was his Rosa Luxembourg with a laptop, Aphrodite with plastic explosive.

When she finished her diatribe with a peroration condemning all multi-national corporations, the military, and the Santos Supermarket chain (it imported lettuce from dictatorial regimes and carried bad canned coffee from plantations in Central America which exploited the peasants), she stopped and looked at her watch.

"I have to make a phone call," she said, and pulled out a bright blue smartphone, punching in the number with authority. "Mali, please," Zera said, and in a moment had begun an animated conversation about some article she was preparing for the *Twelfth Street Liberator*.

When she finished, she explained, "Mali is one of the editors; I was trying to keep her from making my three-thousand-word story into a seven-hundred-word sidebar."

Gordon imagined the offices of the *Liberator*, with pictures of Che Guevara and Castro, Marx and Lenin, and thought of Mali as some tall, comely, cocoa skinned black woman whose parents had named her, in a burst of pride, after an African country that had freed itself from colonial rule.

"I know we have different theories, but the same interest. Will you help me or what?" Zera said.

"I guess, if I can," he answered.

"Great!" she said, reaching over to squeeze his arm. "I know you're not a criminal and together we can find out who is."

Whatever that gesture might have meant to anyone else in the world, to Gordon it meant he had some kind of chance with this woman.

They agreed to meet again when he would bring notes on all the academics who had registered an opinion on the amphora since the day Fontana announced his finding. Together Zera and Gordon would analyze the list to determine who would have the motive and opportunity to seize the vase.

"You really don't think it could just be some crackhead who stumbled into the building, forced Longstreet to open the safe, took the vase, and left him to his heart attack?" Gordon asked.

"That's television," Zera answered, "and racist, too. It's the way cops think. Crack addict equals black guy from Harlem. No, I think you'll find our thief is a white academic with a trick up his sleeve, maybe even mentally unstable due to an obsessive fixation on something." She took a piece of paper out of her purse and wrote those words down. "Save this for when the case is cracked; I will gloat then."

Gordon took the paper, and as he took leave of her, he thought all this would at least give him time to be with her. They were different, but he believed things like this often worked out in real life because he had read about them working out in books.

He walked to the subway to take the train home after leaving Zera, stopping to use the ATM. As he drew out eighty dollars and knew it would be gone in two days, he longed with unexpected nostalgia for the times he would take Jane Freymiller out to an art-house movie and buy a snack afterward for a total expenditure of no more than thirty dollars. New York was devouring him like a frat boy with a Friday night pizza; he had a sense of foreboding about anything and everything facing him then.

He felt less crestfallen as he read in his apartment that night. He considered again what topic he would choose for a dissertation. He thumbed through his well-worn copy of Herodotus' *The Histories* and thought how much he loved it, and Fontana be damned, he would find an adviser willing to allow him to do what interested him. Was being interesting the opposite of being scholarly, he asked himself? The story of Candaules, King of Lydia was his favorite, and he thought deeper than a mere anecdote. Candaules was enamored of his own wife, constantly telling his bodyguard Gyges how beautiful the queen was. Feeling Gyges didn't believe him, he ordered him to hide behind the bedroom door and watch the queen undress for bed, then slip out unnoticed when she turned her back. But the queen caught sight of him, and then flushed out of Gyges who had put him up to it. To preserve her honor she told him there was only one way out to avoid being killed: for him to kill Candaules, take the throne, and marry her. Horrified, but realizing death was the only other possibility for refusing, he obeyed. Beyond its titillation, Gordon thought there was a power dynamic there that the ancients knew about.

Herodotus was from Halicarnassus, Gordon mused, so perhaps this vase and Herodotus' *Histories* could somehow converge into a respectable dissertation topic, making it interesting as well as erudite.

"I want to write something people will read," he said out loud. It didn't occur to him then how childish that statement was; that no one except a few people in a particular field cared a bit for a dissertation.

The next day it was announced at the Penniman that a funeral service for Dr. Longstreet would be held the following Tuesday at the Columbia chapel. He called Zera to tell her and she said they should both attend.

"Sometimes in mystery stories, the killer turns up as a mourner," she said. "We've got to check it out."

On Sunday morning he went out to get *The New York Times*. As he went around the corner to the store, Gordon began to whistle.

Various people on the sidewalk who passed him stared with disbelief or even hostility, as if his happiness and the ability to express it were doing injury to their darker thoughts.

The Ululistani men were just coming in when Gordon returned; they drove taxis and had worked all night. They carried bags of food with them and would cook a huge meal for later in the day.

"You would like to have dinner with us, yes?" one said beseechingly. Gordon's first impulse was to decline, but curiosity and a wish not to spend Sunday alone found him agreeing.

"You come at five o'clock, "one said. "We are neighbors for a long time and don't know each other. Not the same in our country, but in America, yes?"

"Yes, sadly," Gordon admitted. "See you at five."

He went to his apartment and read the paper, considering whether to bring wine but realizing that even if they were only half-hearted Muslims it would be a social blunder even too great for the likes of him.

He went out to a gourmet shop and bought a small box of candy; he knew of no religion that prohibited chocolate. At five o'clock he put on a clean shirt and went down to apartment 3-D and knocked on the door. When it opened, a face with a mustache peeked out and greeted him.

"Ah, yes, our guest," he said, and beckoned Gordon inside.

"I am Hamid," the man said, "and this is Ali, and over there Khalil."

"Hello," Gordon said, shaking hands and returning their half bows with ones of his own.

The kitchen was a steamy battlefield of cooking rice combined with the wafting smells of chicken, lamb, currants, eggplant, lemons, saffron, apples, and onions.

"You sit and rest," Khalil said. He looked like Hamid, except shorter and darker. They were cousins as it turned out, and Ali was a cousin of another cousin.

"You study at Columbia?" Ali said?

"Yes."

"Law"

"No," Gordon replied, and started to answer but they took turns guessing: medicine, business, or perhaps computer science.

"No, classics."

"Classics?" Hamid said blankly.

"The ancient world; Greece and Rome."

"Oh," they said in unison, seemingly dejected that Gordon was aimed in no practical direction.

"Well, no matter," Ali said with a smile, and shortly afterward called them to the table where he was heaping the table with meat and rice delicacies. They prayed for a minute then attacked the food.

"We will tell you about our poor country," they said, and while Gordon ate, they took turns telling about the place of their birth. Ululistan, they explained, was a land that formerly had been part of something that had been part of something else that had been part of the Soviet Union. Ali wiped his fingers, pulled a map from the bookcase, and pointed to a small triangle of earth not far from the Black Sea, south of Armenia, east of Turkey, and north of Iran, that was currently ruled by a despot from whose depravity they hoped to deliver it.

Gordon had vaguely heard of the country, but knew little more. They spoke Ululai, written in Arabic letters but an Indo-European language. The capital was Ululubad, the principal crop Ululi nuts, and the main proverb was a self-hating maxim left over from the days of British colonial rule: "Not bad – for Ululistan."

"We need help in getting our message to people of importance," they said when Gordon had finished his meal. Gordon nearly burst into laughter at their misconception of him as someone worth proselytizing. They gave him a book by their revolutionary leader in exile in England and asked him to read it and pass it along to others.

After playing a tape of native music and serving Gordon a thick, black coffee in a tiny cup, they stood to signal it was time for them to get some rest before going off to work again.

"Thanks so much for a splendid meal," Gordon said.

"We need to cook at home to have our native food," Ali said. "There is only one Ululistani restaurant in New York, and it is in the fold of the UN mission. The villains eat there, a nest of vipers it is. We pass it on Second Avenue, but never go in."

Gordon promised to read the book and walked to the door.

"Okay, cool, fine, totally," Ali said, trying to work all his colloquialisms into one sentence. "One convert today, ten thousand tomorrow."

Gordon shook hands with all of them and trudged upstairs. Later on he telephoned Zera and left a message on her machine. She called back and seemed to enjoy the conversation, although all the while he got the impression that there was someone else in the room with her.

They agreed to meet out in front of the Columbia chapel Tuesday morning before ten to see if any possible suspects were showing their faces. That night Gordon telephoned his parents as he always did on Sundays. He told them about school and his work, and ended by saying, "I think I'm in love but it's too early to tell." He went on and described her as an angel, a wit, a creature of discernment and uniqueness. Of course, he wasn't describing the Zera Alpert of reality, for he hardly knew her. Instead, he was painting a more amazing Zera: the one he had conjured up in his love-addled brain.

He fell asleep that night filled with pleasure at the thought of seeing her again. He hadn't, however, stopped to consider that a date for a funeral was not only a bad idea, but a bad omen.

IV

"A coward dies a thousand deaths,
a brave man only once."

THE SUN BEAT DOWN WITH the strength of mid-summer on Tuesday, the seventeenth of June, the day of Professor Longstreet's funeral. Zera arrived in a black skirt and white blouse whose neck-line suggested more than mourning to Gordon. He wore his only other suit, the dark blue two-button one he had bought before coming east.

"We're appropriately morose," Zera observed, looking at Gordon's clothes and then pointing to herself.

"We're early, too," Gordon said, as only a few people were seated in the chapel, and there was still no sign of a funeral car. Gordon suggested they wait outside to observe mourners as they entered, then take their seats.

After Zera finished her cigarette and checked her watch, a group of faculty members approached from the direction of Low Library. The whole classics department, led by Michael Fontana, was in attendance. Present and former students of the dead man began arriving singly and in groups, and soon after that the president of Columbia University, Sterling Vaughner Pew, Jr., and one of the university chaplains, a rumpled little man with a beard and wire-rimmed glasses who, since he was Unitarian, preferred to be called "Steve" rather than "Reverend Lewes", came across on the asphalt walkway and waited outside the chapel, their academic gowns and colored hoods shifting from time to time in the warm breeze.

In the next few minutes more people seemed to come from every direction, as if they had been awaiting a sign. A black Cadillac hearse pulled into the yard from the Amsterdam Avenue side and stopped by the chapel, followed by several limousines with tinted windows that prevented anyone from seeing the occupants. Unctuous un-dertaker's men opened the doors and gestured with their hands to indicate where people should stand.

Professor Longstreet's widow stood at the front of the family group. Mrs. Longstreet was a once willowy but still shapely ash blonde in the twilight of her attractiveness. Gordon guessed her to be in her mid-fifties. She wore a black dress with sheer black stock-ings that revealed slender, shapely legs. She cried from time to time, dabbing her eyes with a plain white handkerchief. Her two grown children stood with her. A son in his late twenties, who looked like a cheap plaster knock-off of his father, stood with a wife and toddler, while his younger sister, a frizzy haired waif whom Gordon had found out was a semi-perpetual graduate student of French literature at Duke, appeared mildly sedated. Brothers and cousins of the dead professor stood further back.

The hearse door was finally opened and a bronze-colored casket was brought out and set up on a rolling stand by the chapel entrance. President Pew took Mrs. Longstreet's arm and escorted her into the chapel when the signal was given, and the mourners followed. When they were all seated, the pallbearers brought the casket down the aisle. Having surveyed everyone who entered, Zera tugged at Gordon's sleeve and beckoned him to follow her. They slipped in and took their seats at the back.

An organ played a sort of non-denominational antiphon, an inoffensive Corelli-like melody, followed by a standard processional piece from the organist's repertoire. When the last notes of music groaned their way out of the old instrument, the chapel fell silent. A muffled cough and the squeak of a chair preceded Reverend Steve's rising from his seat to begin the service. He recited a short prayer that hovered around the subject of death, but did not insist on God, final judgment, or an afterlife, leaving it politely indeterminate and up to each listener how much they wished to project or believe in an existence beyond this worldly sphere. He then sped through an epistle of St. Paul, almost with embarrassment to Gordon's way of thinking, as if something by John Keats, John Lennon, or the Bhagavad Gita would have been more hip. Michael Fontana read a section of Homer in Greek, then English, sighing and emoting in the places he thought the original bard must have placed the emphasis, trying to create in the listeners' ears a hint of the Aeolian harp and the lapping waves of the wine-dark sea.

Gordon, although a mostly lapsed Catholic, had a sudden yearning for vestments, incense, and a somber choir bellowing out the *Dies Irae*. Modern religion, he concluded, in an attempt to be relevant, only wound up being insignificant.

When it was time for a eulogy, President Pew stood and praised Longstreet as a kindly teacher, a learned scholar, and a friend. He spoke clearly and articulately, mesmerizing Gordon with the flashes from his expensive cufflinks as he raised his arms now and again to make a point. He spoke with such an imitation of sincerity that even those who knew him believed he had written the words himself and possibly meant some of them.

The recessional was Chopin's *Marche Funebre*, which even by Gordon's classical tastes was too depressing.

Zera leaned over and whispered in his ear, "Music for dead Hapsburgs."

When the service was over and the mourners had marched out behind the casket, Mrs. Longstreet stood ready to greet them on the chapel steps. When Gordon introduced himself as a student and her husband's assistant at the Penniman, Mrs. Longstreet took both his hands, then spontaneously leaned forward and kissed him more on the side of the mouth than his cheek, smearing him with lipstick and saliva nearly to the ear lobe as he tried to turn away. The smell of spirits, gin he thought, also came forth in the kiss.

"Come and see me, Gordon, please," she said as she released him. "We have a lot to talk about."

Gordon was sure she confused him with some dissertation advisee of her husband's, but he said he would call, and stepped back to find Zera at the edge of the crowd.

"I've been checking them all out, but I haven't seen anything suspicious," she said with disappointment.

Gordon watched the casket being loaded into the hearse and the mourners dispersing. The daylight was piercing and the sky perfectly blue. Manhattan seemed to burst with energy as the sun approached its meridian position, cruelly, Gordon thought, moving on from a momentary commemoration of the dead to the endless, mindless bustle of those left living.

"I'm starved," Zera said, breaking Gordon's contemplation. "Let's find a place to eat where we can sort this out."

They walked toward Broadway and headed south until they passed the aroma of an open hearth and barbecue.

"This smells good," Zera said and stopped suddenly. *The Tangiers* was a dimly lit café with appealing food and white tablecloths, and they went inside. Large, hammered pewter plates decorated the walls, as well as color prints of dervishes, sultans, and harem girls. Gordon's appetite had returned, but he was a poor second to Zera who devoured bread and hummus as soon as the waiter brought it. She ordered skewered lamb, while Gordon chose the chicken kebab with rice and chickpeas.

She sat across from him and took her tablet out. In between bites she began writing down things she and Gordon knew about the amphora, the controversy surrounding it, the people who had proximity to the treasure, and the security arrangements.

"I think I know how much it is worth," Gordon said

"How much?" she asked, pencil at the ready.

"More than fifty thousand dollars, perhaps even several hundred thousand."

Zera frowned. "I still doubt money was the motive. The vase was stolen to keep the myth alive."

Gordon listened to her latest take on a conspiracy, but his mind soon lost its powers of concentration as he stared into her eyes and kept thinking how he could casually invite her to his place for dinner. He started to speak but lost his courage when he was unable to interrupt her.

"How could we go about baiting these people into tipping their hand? That is what we need to figure out," she wondered out loud.

When they had finished their meal, the waiter took Gordon's money as quickly as a shark ate small fish. Zera and Gordon walked to the door, and once they were on the sidewalk, Gordon knew he had to speak.

"When can I see you again?" he asked.

"Friday," she said hastily. "That's when I have an interview with Fontana. I'll be here on campus at three. Why don't I call you as soon as I'm done?"

He was so elated by this that he was sure he was blushing, but she said a hasty goodbye and made for the subway. Perhaps his luck was about to change, he thought. He knew she would be difficult to win, that she was probably more in love with Che Guevara, Nietzsche, or even John Malkovich, anyone with more derring-do than a classics student. But he was hopelessly infatuated, and even though she talked nonsense half the time, there was confidence and certainty in the way she expressed herself that he wished he could emulate. If she could be so convinced of so much, surely, he could learn to be that way about a little.

When Gordon got back to the Penniman, Detective Sabatini was there waiting for him, as well as someone from the Columbia campus police named Hanrahan, a heavy-set man with bushy eyebrows who let the detective do the talking.

"Some more questions," Sabatini said offhandedly, and took Gordon to Longstreet's office. Professor Fontana was in the hallway and stared at them for a moment before nodding slightly to Sabatini. Gordon for some reason thought of Caesar's last moment watching Brutus smile politely while fingering the dagger under his toga.

"I've been examining everyone's comings and goings from the time the am-fow-ra was last seen," Sabatini began, pronouncing the

Greek word like a man with a mouth full of dental instruments. "And as nearly as I can establish, there were only four people who could have stolen it if it was an inside job."

Gordon froze then, realizing that all the idle speculations about who did it were now devolving into a theory.

"Professor Longstreet was the curator and had virtually unlimited solo access – a shabby bit of security if I do say so – but he's dead so I can't question him. Which isn't to say I exclude him, but for now he's not going anywhere. Next is Professor Fontana, who had custody of the thing for his study and lecture, but for that reason seems to be without any motive for its disappearance if it made him look bad for the safe to be empty as he was about to speak. Then there's the security guard who could have rummaged through enough things to have found the combination, but he's retired NYPD, so I doubt that. Lastly, there's you, and don't take this the wrong way, but you're a living-on-the-edges graduate student with no money. If that was the motive, I'd have to put you in first place as a suspect."

Sabatini rolled his unlit cigar in his mouth and watched Gordon's face. Gordon, always overly sensitive, could feel his color rising.

"I've never stolen anything in my life," he said.

"I'm going to read you your rights now," the detective said. "You have a right to remain silent…"

He rolled through the Miranda warning that Gordon had heard so often on television. When he was done, Gordon said, "I have nothing to hide; I'll tell you anything about myself you want to know."

Sabatini didn't respond to that but began his interrogation.

"I'm going to ask you to take me through all the places you were the day the am-fow-ra disappeared," he said.

Gordon walked him through the small office where he examined and labeled shards of pottery, the secretary's office, the viewing rooms, the cupboards, and finally the auditorium where the lecture was held. Hanrahan followed silently but stared at Gordon all the time.

"That's it?" Sabatini said when Gordon stopped talking.

"Yes, that's it."

Sabatini looked at his notes. "I have at least one eyewitness who said you left at noontime for lunch with a young black guy."

Gordon was stunned and denied it, asking who had said that.

"I'm not at liberty to disclose," Sabatini said.

The detective took Gordon up to the second level of the Penniman and walked to the men's room. Once inside he went to a framed wooden window which had a grill, and as Sabatini demonstrated, it was not fastened tightly to the window frame. Two turns of a bolt loosened it enough to see how it could be pushed away.

"One way the missing object could have left the building is by someone lowering it out this window to a confederate below, perhaps in a sack tied to a rope," Sabatini said.

"But the vase was locked in the safe until the time of the lecture."

"Maybe, maybe not. Someone who had the combination might have taken the vase earlier, and the shock of seeing it missing maybe caused Longstreet to have a heart attack. The medical examiner has said he died sometime in the morning and apparently laid there until their search of the building found him about seven thirty P.M." He paused and added, "Is it lay, laid, or lain? I never get that right."

"Lay, I think is the one you want," Gordon replied.

"Right, "Sabatini said

They returned to Gordon's desk and Sabatini thumbed through his notebook. Gordon's mouth went dry and he began to perspire.

"I'd like you to come with me now to the station for some questions."

"I have nothing to conceal," Gordon said.

"Good, then let's take a ride."

Hanrahan prepared to take leave of them, but turned to Gordon and said, "The university is likely going to take some administrative action in your case while the investigation progresses."

"What kind of action?"

"I will leave that up to the graduate school to decide," he replied and walked away.

Gordon left the Penniman with Sabatini, who had parked his beat-up four-year-old black sedan at the Amsterdam Avenue gate. A police cadet in a khaki uniform was writing a ticket as Sabatini approached.

"Geez, this is funny," Sabatini laughed, taking his cigar out of his mouth. "You've gotten this far in training and you don't know a detective vehicle?"

The cadet kept writing and Sabatini swore at him.

"I'm on the job, dipshit," he said, and opened the back door for Gordon.

"I can have you arrested for…," the rookie began, but Sabatini pulled out his badge, and the cadet folded his ticket book and skulked away. Sabatini sped north to 134th Street where the precinct house was located.

Once inside, Sabatini took Gordon to a small room with faded green walls and went through the days leading up to Longstreet's death and the theft of the vase. For an hour and a half he asked

Gordon about his life, his finances, and his relationships with people in the classics department.

When Sabatini had finished, he stood and hiked up his pants.

"You're free to go," he said abruptly.

Gordon exhaled with relief and walked to the door.

"Don't leave town without letting me know," he said.

'"Are you satisfied I'm not involved with any crime?" Gordon asked, detesting the near whimper in his voice.

"In a word: no," Sabatini answered.

"Have you investigated whether someone interested in embarrassing Professor Fontana might have taken the amphora?"

Sabatini glared at him. "Are you going to tell me how to investigate a crime?"

"Zera Alpert, the reporter from *The Liberator* who was here that night thinks that…"

"Oh, please," the detective said cutting him short. "That broad calls me every other day and says there is a conspiracy on the part of some other professors to steal the vase to keep Fontana's theory from being accepted."

"And you don't think that's a possibility?"

"No, because I have a much better theory; you or someone like you popped it for the dough, and I'm going to find out who it was."

Gordon left the station house and walked back to his apartment in a funk. He couldn't imagine who could have said he was with a young black man. The words "mistaken identity" and "wrongly accused" kept coming to his lips.

On the corner of Broadway and 125th Street Gordon waited for the traffic light to change. A man in a greasy sports jacket and dirty chinos, with shoes untied, tousled hair, and a knapsack on his back, was taking salvage from one of the trash barrels. As Gordon and the other pedestrians waited, the man pulled out a glass bottle and two soda cans, and then with nothing visible but paper and other trash, he picked through more debris before finding another bottle. When the search required moving more things, he began tossing, then angrily throwing anything that was not a redeemable object. Paper bags, plastic food containers, and cardboard flew through the air to the street. A bus was stopped at the intersection, and the man flung an old collapsed umbrella at it, then more cardboard, and lastly a single sneaker. Bystanders looked at this wanton littering, but no one spoke to the man, who had such a fearful single-mindedness to his expression, grimacing and grunting with anger, that no one knew if he was merely vexed or bordering on homicidal.

The light changed and Gordon crossed the street, sidestepping the trash, and walked double time the rest of the way to his apartment. Once there he called Zera.

"I think I'm in trouble," Gordon said, and in a thousand rambling words summarized his afternoon with the detective.

"Why did you say so much to him without a lawyer present?" Zera asked with incredulity in every word.

"Because I'm innocent."

"It's because you're innocent that you need a lawyer."

"I can't afford one."

"Or afford not to," she argued.

"Maybe if I had stolen the amphora, I could pay," Gordon said bitterly.

Zera put him on hold and came back on the line a minute later with a name.

"Harvey Knippelman," she said, and read a phone number.

"He's a cousin of my father and does criminal law. I'll call him now and let him know you'll be in touch."

"I can't pay him."

"You don't have to; I'll front the money."

"I can't ask you to spend your money on me."

"It isn't my money, actually. It all came from my great-grandfather."

"I can't take his money, either," Gordon said.

"He's long dead and left it in a trust fund for me. Did you ever hear of Alpert's Grade A lead pencils?"

"I had them in school," Gordon said with surprise, thinking of the yellow pencils with the pink eraser that had a red "A" on the side.

"Well every time you wrote your ABCs, my family collected some money, so think of it as socialist payback."

"You have a trust fund?" he asked.

"Yes, and if you breathe a word of it, I'll never speak to you again. It discredits me as a true proletarian, but I justify it because it allows me to work for the destruction of capitalism."

"But don't you compromise your journalistic integrity by paying my fees?"

"We're an advocacy publication; we say that right up front and we give money to many causes we write about. Conventional journalism includes tabloids who pay people for their stories, so who's kidding who?"

"Whom," Gordon added, still in a grammatical frame of mind from his time with Sabatini.

"Whatever," Zera said. "Right now you need the Alpert Trust and the *Twelfth Street Liberator* to save your sorry traditionalist ass."

Gordon was amused by that and hung up. He had, he thought, detected a slight tone of endearment in her voice. He waited a short while then called Knippelman who agreed to see him at ten o'clock the following morning. At five o'clock the usual fifteen minutes of music from upstairs came on, and after that it was quiet. He went out to buy some soup, then came home to eat it on his little kitchen table with the radio on playing songs from his time in high school, which set him to thinking he had taken one huge wrong turn in coming to New York. He could have been happy with Jane in Chicago, or even Peoria he thought. Why did he need to prove something to himself in such a complicated place as this? He had romanticized about New York before he came, and still did to some degree, but its size and complexity seemed a challenge in itself before even getting to the demands of school.

Later he wrote down everything he could think of to tell Knippelman, but by doing it became too wound up to sleep, too upset to think about sex with Zera, and too distracted to even read Herodotus. The hours on the clock crept along, and finally he fell asleep around three A.M. His clock radio went off at seven, and he felt as if he had slept on a pile of paving stones. He wasn't scheduled to work that day, but dressed to go downtown to see Knippelman, whose office was near the Flatiron.

The subway ride was punctuated by an argument between two young men who looked as if they had been out all night. When Gordon got off the train at his stop, he half expected to hear the sound of gunfire, but the train pulled away with the two men still arguing but not violently. The smell of the city's overheated refuse rose to greet him as he came up from the subway. Sandwich vendors and street hawkers were setting up for business, and the daily theater of the getting and the spending was in full view.

Gordon found the building address and took the elevator up five floors to enter a suite that said "Law Offices of Greenberg, Hootstein, Knippelman, Mochensen, & O'Brien". He was greeted by a secretary who looked like Lucille Ball and sounded like Yogi Berra. She sat him down and announced his presence in whispered tones over the telephone. In a few moments an older man, perhaps seventy, in a hounds tooth checked jacket and seldom polished leather shoes appeared. He smiled a smile of weariness and resolution.

"Harv Knippelman," he said, his lips parting to reveal old, yellowing teeth under a thin mustache. He jerked Gordon's arm up and down like a pump handle.

Gordon was shepherded inside to a room with a long table and handsomely bound law books, two telephones, numerous awards and diplomas, and pictures of Harvey with all the former New York mayors going back to Koch. Koch hogged the picture, Dinkins looked sedated, Giuliani ebullient, Bloomberg confident, and de Blasio resigned to a short time in office. There was no picture of Adams, however, a reproach that implied Knippelman wasn't important enough to have met him yet but continued to hope.

"So it seems you have a problem here," Harvey began, and summarized what Zera had told him. "Legal services aren't cheap, but because you are a friend of Zera's, we'll cut you a discount. Say four hundred dollars an hour."

Gordon gasped audibly and began to cough. Harvey poured him a glass of water.

"Zera is going to fund the retainer, so let's focus on the case, not the expense."

Gordon told him of Hanrahan's comment about some university action.

"I suspect they will suspend you either as an employee or a

student so you can't come and go from the crime scene while they investigate."

Gordon felt a coldness in his gut and perspiration running from under his arms.

"Tell me everything, starting from the very beginning," the attorney said.

Gordon filled in the details about the amphora, Longstreet's death, and Sabatini's inclination to make him the most likely suspect. Knippelman then explained the penalties for grand larceny and gave him some advice on when a detective would go from suspecting a person to placing him under arrest.

"He needs something more tangible at this point. You were there and about, you had opportunity. Also motive in a general way, money, but that isn't enough. Anyone who worked in the building could probably fall under the same suspicion. What he needs is some concrete piece of evidence to link you to the theft."

"Oh," Gordon said, unsure whether he should take that as happy news.

"There isn't anything else I should know, is there?" Harvey said, leaning across the table and folding his hands prayerfully, looking Gordon directly in the eye.

Gordon mentioned what Sabatini had said about the young black man which elicited no reaction.

"Not that I care one way or another, but I have to ask," Harvey pronounced in a sad voice. "Did you steal it?"

Gordon felt bereft of a friend in the world then. He had not convinced Harvey apparently, who sat there as stone-faced as a gargoyle on a cathedral.

"No, I didn't."

"Standard procedure," the lawyer said, waving a hand as if to erase the question.

Harvey stood and shook Gordon's hand, walking him to the front desk. He handed him a card and told Gordon to call, particularly if Sabatini arrested him.

"Do you think that will happen?" Gordon said in shock.

"The police generally like to arrest people for things like this," Harvey said. "It's kind of what they do. If someone else doesn't emerge as a better suspect, I think they will turn back to you."

Gordon said goodbye to Harvey and walked past Lucille Ball, who was eating a jelly donut that had leaked onto the copy of the *New York Post* on her desk.

Gordon returned home and sat at his kitchen table for a long time. Instead of going back to Illinois as a conquering hero, it might be as a parolee. He had been the bright academic star, but if he were charged with a crime, he would be known as the family failure, the black sheep of whom no one spoke.

The next morning he called Zera to let her know what had happened, but that he didn't see how Harvey could help him, only represent him if he was charged.

"Then you have to take matters into your own hands, Gordon."

"How?"

"That's the whole point. No one can tell you how. You have to figure it out for yourself. It's like asking someone how to be resourceful. It needs to come from you."

"Then I guess I would have to catch the criminal myself if the police aren't of a mind to look further than me."

"Bingo, my lad. Right answer."

Gordon went to work later that morning, but when he got to

his desk at the Penniman, a security guard told him he would have to report to the dean's office. Gordon shrugged and walked across the campus to the basement level of the Low Library where he was ushered into Dean Aimer's suite. The dean sat with another man whom he introduced as one of the university's deputy general counsel. Gordon decided this did not involve his most recent amended request for more financial aid.

Gordon attempted humor, looking at the dean while saying, "You look stern."

The dean registered surprise, and the lawyer said, "Actually I am Stearn. Josh Stearn."

Gordon thought he must have seen the name somewhere and hence the joke was bad free association on his part.

"Mr. Bauer," the dean began. "We are faced with a rather unusual set of circumstances. Our security department and the New York police are apparently considering you a prime suspect in the amphora theft."

"But I didn't do it," Gordon said, in a way that sounded like a tinny repetition of all his previous denials.

Dean Aimer went on as if he hadn't heard what Gordon said.

"We must, under the circumstances, order your employment at the Penniman suspended until the investigation is complete."

"But I haven't been formally charged or arrested," Gordon protested.

"No, but you might be," Dean Aimer said with too much cheer in his voice.

"But right now I'm entitled to the presumption of innocence."

The dean looked at his legal counsel who shook his head from side to side.

"That's only in a court of law," Josh Stearn said. "The university has the right to suspend any criminal during an employee investigation…, I mean EMPLOYEE during a CRIMINAL investigation." He blushed a bit at his juxtaposition of the words.

"And we are suspending you indefinitely as of this moment," Aimer added.

"For what exactly?" Gordon cried.

"Because you are under suspicion."

"Suspicion of what?"

The dean hesitated, stammering for a moment, then said, "You are under suspicion of, well, ah, being a suspect."

Aimer explained that Gordon was still an enrolled student who could attend classes and use the library, but he was barred from Mandeville Hall and the Penniman.

As he left the dean's office, he realized he was the only one who could clear his name since no one else seemed very interested in the project. For once he had to step outside the persona of the institutional naif who never questioned authority. Now he needed to break the rules, play the rebel, and save his own hide. He thought of Humphrey Bogart and Sean Connery, men who would not take this lying down if it were happening to them.

He felt overwhelmed by New York, and even more so by his own ineptitude at life. He had chosen a career he realized now was not according to what he liked or disliked, but what he felt he *ought* to be doing.

"Dangerous word, that 'ought'", a history professor at Loyola had once said. "Heads are cut off, wars started, countries ruined, all for a simple five-letter word that implies what you are doing isn't quite right enough."

Gordon pondered that for a moment as he walked. All his thoughts had been derived from his parents, religion, and school. He could not imagine something he really wanted to do, or having the courage to act on it. "Gnothi seauton; Know thyself" was the old Greek ideal, but his own self was the subject he was most in the dark about.

It disturbed him to realize he was as old as he was, but in the ways of the world, as stupid as a wicker basket. Now that had to change. An old Latin proverb came to mind: "Tene lupum auribus."

"Take the wolf by the ears," he said, while knowing that translating it into action would be harder than into English.

"If you have to ask, you can't afford it."

THE BEST BUZZ COFFEE SHOP on Broadway at 112th Street was filled the next morning. The bumble bee on their logo, perched on the rim of a coffee cup, looked down on the hopelessly hooked who were lined up for their morning drinks, not unlike a methadone clinic that Gordon had passed once. The Best Buzz clientele was more nattily attired, but no less dependent. Gordon mulled his situation over a plastic cup of iced mocha latte. He was in a twilight zone of not being thought innocent, but not convicted either.

Gordon watched the espresso bar operator spin out the orders as they were given to him by the cashiers. Small strainers for coffee were wrenched into place on the exquisite Italian espresso machine. Blasts of steam turned milk into froth while the operator banged out the grounds, mixed, stirred, and spooned substances into or onto drinks in a blizzard of activity before handing the cup to a waiting customer. It was art in the service of commerce, he thought. A plain, pre-war ten-cent cup of joe never satisfied anyone so much as a five-dollar boutique drink.

"You have to find something that proves your innocence," Zera had told him over the phone that morning. "Or something that proves someone else's guilt."

He pondered that notion as he looked down at the table where a manila folder lay. A fifteen-page mnuscript that he had written was waiting for a decision. As a break from strict academic work in the spring semester, he had researched the topic of eccentric academic personalities in history and was ready to submit it to journals and magazines. It seemed a clever way to break into print, but now he considered whether the lack of humor in academe would find what he wrote to be evidence of heresy. Bad enough to be a suspected felon, but a buffoon on top of it would eliminate any chance of a career. He thought some more, then drank down his coffee, and finally went next door to the Copy-Copy shop to have multiple copies made to mail out to editors. If he was going down on a sinking ship, what further harm could there be?

"Hello," he said at the counter to a woman whose name badge, a piece of adhesive tape over someone's name badge, said "Jill".

"What can I do for you, chief?" she said, snapping her chewing gum at the end of the sentence.

Gordon took out the manuscript and asked for twenty copies.

"Collated, stapled?"

"Whatever," Gordon replied, mesmerized by her strong profile and red hair. If Zera was unavailable, perhaps he should look elsewhere.

"Well, one or both?"

"Collated, no staples," he sighed.

She turned to one of the copy machines and inserted the pages, hit a few buttons, and it proceeded to spit out copies into bins.

Gordon looked at the woman's hands. She wore rings on most of her fingers, but none that looked like a wedding band or engagement ring. But then it occurred to him that a woman in black slacks, a strawberry-colored T-shirt with Janis Joplin's image, and a gold stud in her nose would not be wearing anything as conventional as a wedding ring.

"I'm taking my break after this," she shouted to the manager who was at the other end of the counter. He nodded, and when she was done, she put Gordon's copies in a box and took his money without a glance back at him.

He walked from the counter and waited by the door, pretending to examine his copies, look at his watch, and wait for "Jill" to leave for her break, which he assumed would be to go to Best Buzz. He would seize the moment and ask her to join him for a cappuccino, although he felt himself at dangerous levels of caffeine intake already. He would be smooth and suave; it would all go in such a natural flow, he thought.

"May I ask you," he said, speaking up, just at the same moment another young woman came through the door, gave "Jill" a kiss on the lips, took her hand, and started leading her out the door.

"You wanted to ask something?"

Gordon coughed and spoke, "Does stapling cost extra?"

"No, it's all in the same price."

Gordon watched as the two women went next door, and he proceeded to walk in the opposite direction wondering how he did not consider that "Jill" was gay. Not that one could tell by appearance, he corrected himself correctly, except that people in New York all seemed to have "gaydar" as they called it, and could calibrate their targets accordingly. Gordon always seemed to be in the dark as to who was gay, lesbian, or even transsexual. He had an older cousin, Claudia Hindemuth, who came back from college one Christmas and announced she was gay, but she turned out to be only a Smith College sophomore-year experimental lesbian, and later married William Gessler and had two children right away. It was all too perplexing for Gordon.

Back at his flat he opened a can of ravioli and decided to put the article on the shelf for a while. If he exonerated himself he might send it out, but for now, he had to work on the first matter. The phone rang and it was Zera, which delighted him even though they spoke of nothing personal.

"I was talking with Darwin, my publisher, about this today and he knows someone who collects these Greek antiquities," she said hurriedly. "Darwin comes from money and went to prep school and college with this guy who came from money and works on Wall Street making even more money...," and she took a breath. "Anyway: point being, he's a big time player and knows a great deal. We can talk with him if you want. Darwin says he could fill us in on how amphoras are bought and sold, and what an art thief or common criminal would have to do to unload one."

"It might convince you I'm right," Gordon said in a tone of triumph.

"Nothing could persuade you that you are wrong, though, and that's where we differ," Zera retorted.

She said she would make arrangements, and two days later she called and told him to be at Fifth Avenue and Seventieth Street at six o'clock. When he got there Zera was waiting, smoking a cigarette and pacing, even though Gordon was ten minutes early.

"The guy's rich as Croesus, I understand," Zera said. "We'll have a chance to see a part of New York reserved for *Architectural Digest.*"

"What part of New York is that?"

"A townhouse with an art collection," she said nonchalantly.

They walked a block east and stopped in front of a wonderfully elegant private residence. Zera rang the bell, waited for a voice to come to the intercom, and then announced herself. She and Gordon were buzzed in, but then found themselves in a small foyer facing an internal front door made of bronze. The door behind them clicked locked, and they saw they were contained in their space as several security cameras viewed them. After ten seconds, the bronze door swung open and a man in an athletically cut suit asked to see identification, and then led them into a reception area whose focal point was a painting of Madonna and Child by Giotto. He called someone on a phone and then took them to the elevator, which rode them up to the third floor.

Another security man stood waiting for them when the door opened and took them to the library, where a bespectacled man in a tuxedo with an immaculate white dinner jacket and an amazing mane of hair stood to greet them. He introduced himself as "Robertson", but Gordon was too embarrassed to ask if that was his first or last name. The library was filled with expensively bound books, framed maps and autographs, and several display cases with pottery, gold and silver work, and two Greek amphoras.

"I do have to be at the Metropolitan for an event in about an hour," he said apologetically, but I'll try to fill you in on what you might want to know about buying and selling art objects."

He offered them a drink, then poured some whisky into three

glasses before they had a chance to decline. "I've had a hectic day," he said as he took a sip.

"Where do you work?" Gordon said chattily.

"On the street," the man said.

Gordon figured that meant Wall Street, not selling souvenirs in Times Square.

"Do you trade stocks?" Zera asked, the tone of her voice rising as if she were about to confront an actual capitalist and pummel him with Marxist ideology.

Robertson shook his head. "No, I do deals."

"What kinds of deals?" Gordon asked earnestly.

"Oh, today we collateralized Uruguay, took Montenegro public, and merged the Vatican with General Motors," he said with a smile. "That sort of thing."

Gordon would have liked to ask him more questions about a world he knew nothing of, but Robertson took them to a corner where an amphora sat in a glass case.

"Did Darwin tell you all about the theft at Columbia?" Zera asked.

"Yes," Robertson said, "and that this poor fellow might be under suspicion because he worked there."

"But he didn't do it," Zera said.

"I guess not, or I'd be a fool to have him here," Robertson laughed.

He went on to explain the relative value of amphoras that had been used for ordinary purposes like wine or olive oil, and hence could be unearthed all over Greece, Asia Minor, and Sicily. "Most people don't know the Greeks were everywhere from the Western

Mediterranean to Turkey. My two are from Corinth and Athens and aren't particularly rare."

"Where did you buy the vases?" Gordon asked.

"Oh, I don't. I just steal them," Robertson said.

"Now I know you are joking, "Zera said.

"Yes, but I can see why people do steal them; the prices of them and all art objects seem to continually increase. One of mine belonged to my grandfather, the other I got at auction at Sotheby's. I haven't gone into the issue of claims by Greece and other countries for return of plundered objects. I have authenticated records of purchase going back a hundred years, but who knows beyond that."

Zera stared at the vase, studying the figures of men who had been stuck in their places for thousands of years.

"Could someone successfully fence one?"

"I suppose, although the risk is large and the reward small. Any dealer knowingly taking stolen goods could be ruined, and it isn't like gold which can be melted down. The ultimate purchaser is usually a collector or museum who would demand to know the provenance, although that could be faked by someone who knows the scene."

"I hear that art objects are sometimes stolen to order," Gordon said.

"That's true," Robertson said, "but amphoras are pretty common; they aren't Rembrandts."

With that, he went to the bookshelf and took down a large, illustrated book on Greek pottery, turning the pages for Gordon and Zera to see some examples of different styles.

Zera toyed with a strand of hair and shifted her weight to one leg, half turning as if in thought. "So if the monetary gain isn't that great and selling it would be difficult, could it have been stolen for some other reason, say to make a political point?"

"I suppose anything is possible these days," Robertson said, looking at his watch. "I hope I was of some help."

"A great deal of help," Zera said, and they all shook hands.

The security man came when Robertson pressed a button and escorted them downstairs and outside.

"Well, at least we have seen how the one percent lives; I looked him up before we came, and he is estimated to have earned two hundred million dollars last year. He was Darwin's Princeton roommate, and Darwin I know has family money; that's how the *Liberator* is financed."

Gordon thought he was surely the only person in Manhattan without money, and that in itself was tantamount to crime. He had believed all his life that poverty was virtue of a sort, especially if it was voluntary, the kind teachers and social workers embraced. Here it more and more seemed a disability if not a disaster.

"What do you propose we do now? " Gordon asked.

Zera looked at him intently. "I don't think we have too much time to work on alternative theories. Perhaps the only way for us to go is to take two positions simultaneously. I will help you look for evidence that it was a common crime if you agree to help me track down some of the possible ideological conspirators I think are behind this."

"I accept," he said, being agreeable to anything she would propose.

As they stood there in front of the banker's townhouse, a Mercedes Benz sedan pulled up and the banker exited his home and stepped into the car, accompanied by one of the security men and an elegant woman in an evening dress. They drove off in the direction of Fifth Avenue and the museum. Zera and Gordon walked through Central Park and saw a group of evening joggers assembling for their run. They were white and affluent, men and women fresh from busy days practicing law or analyzing investments, with a few computer geeks thrown in for good measure. They were thin to borderline anorexic, with bony faces and pelvises protruding through their running shorts, their knees, elbows, and collarbones all visible. Each had the look of the zealot. Two men jogged into the park and joined them, shouting, "We've already gone three, hurry up."

"Some of us have to work," one runner rejoined.

"So much the pity," one of the early runners said, perspiration on his face and wet marks on his shirt.

The newcomers joined them and they all ran off in the direction of the reservoir. Gordon thought their healthiness was more appalling than being unfit. They had a drawn look to them, and a religious fervor which would have bade them cast their eyes away from cheesecake, much less eat any.

The rest of the park was filled with baby-strolling nannies, skateboarders, and dog walkers. He looked at the women he saw and felt he was unsuited to any of them. He lacked a pedigree, a fine apartment, and self-confidence.

Zera said good-bye when they reached the west side of the park; she was off to a press conference at the health department where high-fat diets were being targeted.

"On the one hand, better food is better, but banning burgers and soft drinks punishes the proletariat, not the ruling class who can afford gyms, spas, and special diets," she grumbled, lighting a cigarette, having two puffs, then putting it out in her relentless battle to quit. She flagged down a cab, and Gordon asked why she didn't take the subway.

"It's hot, dirty, and crowded," she said, jumping into the taxi.

As it sped off, he thought how much she loved the workers of the world in the abstract, but didn't want to be shoulder to shoulder with them. He remembered a quote from Stendhal: "I love the people, I hate their oppressors, but it would be a perpetual torture for me to live with the people…I had, I still have the most aristocratic tastes. I would do everything for the happiness of the people, but I would sooner, I believe, pass two weeks of every month in prison than live with shopkeepers." Gordon somewhat agreed and was honest enough to admit it. Champagne socialism was the best way to be egalitarian.

He walked north, wanting fresh air even though it would take him three-quarters of an hour to get home. A shapely redheaded college girl whisked past Gordon on roller skates. Her breasts clung to her moist jersey as the wind blew against her. Her shorts rose up high and with the slits cut along the sides, he caught a partial view of her buttocks as she passed him, leaving in her wake a slight whiff of the scent "Topaz" in his nostrils. It was what Jane Freymiller had worn, and waves of nostalgia swept over him. He longed for those uncomplicated nights with her and wanted to call her, but didn't want to hear that she was dating someone new, and certainly could not bear to reveal his current dilemma to her.

He saw an elderly couple sitting on a bench near Eighty-Eighth Street, and could detect romance even in their eyes. Perhaps this was all a sport he was doomed to fail at, he thought. Like a defeated gladiator about to be eaten by a lion, he felt his knees knocking. He lacked the courage to pursue Zera or anyone and wondered where he might find it.

Once he got home, he was too tired to even feel sorry for himself. After a supper of bacon and eggs, he balanced his checkbook and did his laundry in the dreary basement utility room. He might as well be in jail by the end of the summer because his money was fast running out. Even if he cleared his name, he saw himself returning to Illinois with the word "Failure" tattooed on his forehead.

Later he went to the convenience store and bought a quart of fudge swirl ice cream, eating half of it that night, thinking after he finished that from such beginnings people got to weigh five hundred pounds and be unable to get out of bed or even their rooms. He had a picture in his mind of the fire department coming to break down the doors while a photographer from one of the tabloids snapped a picture to be captioned, "Fat Boy Eats Himself Into Captivity."

Gordon thought of the thousands of lonely people in the city whose sufferings were both like and different from his own. It struck him as amazing that knowing how to make one's way in the world was never taught in any of the schools he had attended. He concluded it was a subject everyone was supposed to learn on his own. Gordon looked out the window and wondered why people were so foolish as to come to New York when New York could succeed in making them look even more foolish still.

He picked up the phone and dialed Jane's number, quickly hanging up, but then redialing. It rang four times and her machine clicked on.

"This is Jane, and I know I'll be happy to hear that you've called. Please leave a message and I will call you back," her voice said, with the familiar Midwestern chirpiness.

Gordon hung up, realizing the only message he could leave would have been, "Jane, this is Gordon. I'm broke and failing, likely to be arrested, infatuated with a woman who doesn't know I'm alive. I miss what we had but still need to figure out what my life is about. Can you wait ten years for me, please?"

He knew what he expected from life was some measure of happiness, and that everything so far was going in the opposite direction; the need to construct a plan B was now, even to a blockhead like himself, transparently obvious.

The next day he walked to the main branch of the public library to look up articles and books on art thefts, hoping it would give him some hope or at least tools to extricate himself from this position of being a prime suspect. What he read was discouraging, though, for the thieves were very smart and many of the crimes were never solved. It seemed to him that if the police suspected him and had no evidence against anyone else, they would proceed on what they had rather than do nothing.

Later in the afternoon he felt hungry and went to McDonald's in Times Square. There were street corner evangelists, tourists with guidebooks, beggars, and even a nearly naked cowboy singing and playing guitar, only to be trumped by a septuagenarian nearly naked cowgirl also with a guitar strategically covering most of her chest. He found out later they were suing one another claiming the other had infringed on copyrighted domains.

When he left McDonald's he looked across the street and saw a military recruiting station. Didn't men in the old days join the French Foreign Legion to get away from legal jams? He had heard of lenient judges offering young criminals the option of joining the army instead of being sentenced. He decided to go in and at least find out if the military would have him; it might give him some bargaining card if he were to be arrested.

He pondered the different branches. He was prone to seasickness, so he ruled out the Navy. He didn't see himself as a fire-eating Marine, either, so he looked at the other posters in the window and entered the building. The Air Force recruiter wasn't there, so by default, he was now sitting in front of an Army sergeant who seemed excited that he had a prospect.

"Sergeant Howe," he said, standing up, shoulders back and ramrod straight, offering his hand to Gordon. The sergeant had decorations and ribbons, badges and pins all over his uniform front, and a demeanor of absolute certainty that Gordon envied.

Gordon told him he was at Columbia but was thinking university life wasn't for him. He left out everything else, and the recruiter didn't seem very interested anyway. They talked for a while, and he said the next step would be for Gordon to report to an army facility for one day for various mental and aptitude tests, as well as a physical. Gordon agreed as there was no obligation beyond that. The sergeant said the army would guarantee certain things like training in a field he showed a particular aptitude for, saying that all the languages Gordon knew would be in his favor.

Gordon left the military office with anxiety, but also some hope that maybe he could dodge all this trouble by enlisting. Perhaps if he were gone, Columbia and the police would lose interest in tracking him down.

"Who said running away was not the way to deal with trouble?" he told himself on the way home, although he had a nagging suspicion that in the electronic age, one's past could never be escaped. He remembered the story of an aristocratic Roman, whose name was placed on a proscription list. He had a nice lakeside house in Alba Longa, and his undoing was that someone put his name on the hit list more out of wish to confiscate the house.

"My Alban villa pursues me," he said when he saw his name on the list.

If a noble Roman could not escape his fate, how could he?

"I vas not a Nazi!"

G ORDON SAT AT HIS KITCHEN table the next morning looking at
a stale package of English muffins and a dirty teacup next to
it, along with the electric bill, two circulars, a flyer from Big Ben's
Yogurt, and yet another handbill from his third-floor neighbors inviting anyone American to attend the next monthly meeting of the
People's Front for the Liberation of Ululistan. As he folded up the
junk mail and began to throw it in the wastebasket, his eye caught
two tickets that were wedged between the salt and pepper shakers.

"The German-American Cultural Society of New York invites
you…" began an invitation notice clipped to the tickets. It was a
dinner dance feted as "Lindenfest", celebrating the flowering of the
scented tree blossoms that were symbolic of summer. Gordon had
purchased the tickets months before in the hope that his romantic
luck would change and he would have someone to take.

He realized it was time to make the bold move. His meetings
with Zera had been so businesslike that it was obvious why she had
not shown signs of being attracted to him. With Jane, love had

happened because she was the one who had planned it. A woman like Zera had so many of her own plans going through her head that Gordon would have to be the architect if any grand structure to his liking were to arise on the spot. He went for the phone and with newfound courage began to dial Zera's number. After the fifth digit, he hung up, feeling a sudden urge to urinate. Once back from the bathroom, he dialed again and she picked up.

"'Lo," she said.

"Zera, Gordon here," he said in his most suave CIA voice. "I was just wondering," he began. "Are you free Saturday night?"

"Yes, what's up?"

"Well, I've got two tickets to a dinner dance on Saturday; would you like to go?"

She was as silent as the sarcophagus of Agamemnon, he thought with a cringe.

"You mean dinner and dancing like a date?"

He was dissolving quickly and stammered, "Yes, but only if you could, and I wouldn't expect you to change plans, but if…"

"Oh, why not?" she interjected.

He was as elated as if she had said yes with enthusiasm. By the time they had gotten off the phone, Gordon had imagined the next two years of their lives together: the dance, a romantic cocktail at midnight, sex of course, courtship, cohabitation, and finally marriage. This business of the stolen amphora would somehow resolve itself.

On Saturday afternoon Gordon laid out the suit he had gotten back from the cleaners, found a starched white shirt in the back of the closet, and a blue tie with the Columbia coat of arms on it that he had bought the first day of school, thinking people at the university actually wore them.

At six o'clock he took the subway downtown to Zera's flat. She was waiting for him at the doorstep. She wore a Chinese-style floral pantsuit, its green silk contrasting nicely with her dark hair, a single-strand necklace, and plain gold earrings. It occurred to him that he had failed to mention that the evening would be on a German theme, although he hardly thought she would have gone out and bought a Bavarian milkmaid's costume.

"Very nicely done up," Gordon said.

"Thank you," she replied, almost with a touch of sweetness. "But you never told me what the occasion is."

"Lindenfest," he began, and she laughed until she realized he meant it.

They cabbed to the East Side and stopped in front of a large townhouse on East 63rd Street. The old brownstone mansion had brightly cleaned glass and a neatly swept walkway with flowers on the border. "The German-American Cultural Society of New York" was on a banner over the door that flapped gently in the summer breeze.

"Holy Toledo," Zera said, covering her face with her hand. "It's the freaking Bund."

Gordon was blushing now, and they got out of the cab and walked to the entrance and into the reception area. Two overstuffed older women at the reception table, one in pale pink, the other sky blue, both with too much makeup and shaking rolls of flesh on their upper arms checked off the names of the arriving guests.

"Herr Bauer," one said, remembering Gordon from their winter solstice concert.

"Guten abend," he answered.

They put on their name tags and went into the ballroom.

"You really speak German?"

"I took it in school, plus my grandmother spoke some from when she was a girl."

"And Greek and Latin?" she asked, seeming impressed.

"And French, with the ability to get through pleasantries in Italian and Spanish," he added, both embarrassed and proud of his sudden immodesty. "Languages come easily to me," he added, thinking to himself, "Except to speak what I really mean to women using standard English."

Zera looked around at the mostly aging population, and she saw in the center of the room there was a reception line for dignitaries. The German ambassador to the UN and the German consul general in New York shook hands with the guests and made small talk. The ambassador was a tall, thin man severe in expression with a long nose which he held high.

"I think I see the ghost of Kurt Waldheim," Zera said.

"German-Americans aren't fascists," Gordon said with slight annoyance.

"Lieutenant Waldheim reporting for duty, sir," Zera said, saluting with one hand and making a mock mustache on her lip with the index finger of the other hand. "I vas only following orders, Herr Hauptmann."

Gordon fell into a state of gloom and embarrassment as they found seats at a circular table and introduced themselves to the people already seated. They were placed with an insurance agent from New Jersey and his wife, two fiftyish sisters from Mamaroneck who sold real estate, an elderly cardiologist with a German accent ("Did he say his name was Mengele?" Zera whispered to Gordon), and a fat man in a canary yellow sports jacket who sweated profusely and ordered beer by the pitcher. The meal was intolerably German for Zera, with wursts and potato salad. A comically antediluvian band played waltzes and oompahs after dinner, and Zera excused herself to go to the ladies' room where Gordon suspected she was lighting up a joint. When she came back Gordon concluded the evening had been the worst disaster since the Hindenberg and said he would take her home.

"You don't want to stay and dance the goose step?" she asked cheerfully.

They left the building at nine-thirty and found themselves in the middle of a perfect summer evening, the sidewalk illuminated by streetlights. Two linden trees were in full bloom, and their scented flowers filled the air with a calm sweetness.

"It's a lovely night; we could walk for a while," Gordon suggested.

They turned onto Madison and went south, the full moon sometimes visible at intersections where it crowned tall buildings. The shops and boutiques were closed, but mannequins in spotlights modeled expensive dresses, fine leather shoes, handbags from Italy, and men's clothing with designer labels, as well as antiques, jewelry, and paintings. Gordon noticed that Zera's head did not turn as she waxed on about her work at the paper, and how she saw it as able to transform society. Capitalism and oppression were the enemies, solidarity and socialism the cure.

"I'm engaged," she said triumphantly.

"To whom?" Gordon asked, gulping down his unhappiness.

"To the cause," she said, realizing then he had misunderstood her. "All other engagements are bourgeois."

He mustered his courage and replied, "And there's no room for emotional attachments?"

She made a face and thrust her hands into her jacket pockets. "There was someone, someone who meant a great deal to me, but it all ended and now I just have to worship from afar."

"How far exactly?"

"Iran, if he's still there. He's a correspondent for *The Guardian*."

"No hope, then?" Gordon said sympathetically.

"For me or Iran?"

"Either."

"I can only speak for myself, and it is no."

They walked for a while in silence and Gordon took her hand.

"I'd like to be considered for the position if you decide to re-post it."

She held his hand for a moment, squeezed it, then let go. "I think you're very sweet, Gordon, but I doubt if I'm what you're looking for."

"I don't know what I'm looking for," he said, "only what I found."

"I am mean through and through, unfit for normal relations."

"So romance is a deviation from your plan to unveil all the wrongs of the world so that they might be corrected," Gordon said.

"No, romance is just a preposterous invention to cheat women out of a real life."

"You can't mean that."

Zera paused and said, 'It's a theory. It depends which day of the week it is whether I believe it or not. My cynicism about love probably stems from my not being good at it."

She changed the subject and asked Gordon why he had gone into classics.

"All the human stories have been told by the ancients: love, war, the cosmic ironies of the universe," he replied.

"But Chinese, Arabic, Persian, and Sanskrit are ancient languages; do you include those traditions in your view of what constitutes wisdom."

"Yes," Gordon said, "of course. I'm traditional but I'm not close-minded. Those languages are classic languages, too, but they have their own departments."

"There's hope for you after all," she said. "You don't think everything important is Western."

"Just most of it," he said.

"Why is it so hard to accept other cultures as possessing wisdom, and that we in the West don't have the right to impose our values on others."

"Yes, like getting judgmental about cannibalism. Silly us; it's just an alternate cultural value," Gordon said.

"You know what I mean," she said.

"I do, and I'll still take the Western tradition before the others."

Gordon went on about Dido and Aeneas, Hero and Leander, Ulysses and Penelope. He believed in love, which despite its bad press, didn't seem to go away. He stopped and stood still, pausing for a moment to lean in and kiss her lightly on the lips. "Keep an open mind on the subject," he said.

"I'm still hungry, "she answered. "Want to find someplace that's open?"

He agreed and they walked to Forty-Ninth to a place with a sign that read "Afro-Cuban Chinese" with a Coca-Cola sign underneath it. They went in and had rice, chicken, and vegetables, and at nearly midnight they left and walked to her flat. She kissed him quickly on the cheek and went up the stairs of her building.

He floated to Broadway to find a cab and arrived home too restless to sleep. He lay in bed thinking of Zera, believing he at least had a chance, until Morpheus finally claimed him for herself. The next day was quiet in the neighborhood. It was Sunday and no one stirred until noon. Even the upstairs music player and the Ululistanis slept late.

Gordon went out to get groceries in the afternoon, walking over to Broadway where there was a natural foods market. He bought fresh vegetables at ruinous prices, fruit, and some barbecued chicken. At the check-out line a Hispanic woman with two small children was struggling to find another quarter for the cashier, while two older gay men were discussing which movie they would like to see that night. Both were dressed in carefully pressed Banana Republic khakis with tropical shirts. An elderly man with terrible dandruff stood in front of another register and shouted "WHAT?" to everything the cashier said. Gordon watched as a young girl stuffed a copy of *People* magazine under her shirt. Two women in their well-preserved forties in running shorts and T-shirts came through the front door and bought small bottles of spring water. Their cheeks were flushed with the exhilaration of their exertions, while the pasty-faced girl at the register stared at them as if they were from Mars, wondering why anyone would work up a sweat for fun. A black man with elegant gold chains on his neck and wrists stood next to a tall, slender woman with cornrow braids. She asked the man questions one after another, to all of which he said, "Uh-huh." When Gordon checked out and started north on Broadway, a group of Hasidic Jews in black, with brimmed hats and side locks, were engaged in a spirited conversation.

As they passed the Copy-Copy shop, a gangly man of indeterminate race with dreadlocks and a plastic trash bag filled with blankets came up to them and rambled on about lost children and the harm to the environment from diesel engines. The Hassidim ignored him and Gordon hurried his pace before the man's arm extended for a handout. Sometimes he gave them money when he had any, but he felt the gates of insolvency were closing on him, and that one day soon he might be the raving man with a plastic bag. He crossed Broadway at 120th and returned to his apartment building, weary although he had only been out one hour. New York, he imagined, must derive its incredible energy by sucking it out of all those who lived there.

Gordon spent the week thinking about what he would do next. There was no word from Sabatini, which gave him hope that he was not the only suspect. Zera invited him downtown for a movie on Thursday, but canceled at the last minute.

"Deadline on a story; sorry," she said, and he fell into a state of gloom until she countered with an offer to take him to lunch on Saturday.

"Sure," he said, with the rapidity of a souse being offered a free drink.

"There's a Central American restaurant in the Village we could try," she said.

When Gordon got to her flat on Saturday, she was sitting in front of her computer screen, the air blue from cigarette smoke, as she worked on a new story.

"It's an expose on how the lottery victimizes poor people, who are the ones buying most of the tickets," she said.

"How can they be victims if they buy them voluntarily?" Gordon asked.

Zera fumed. "That's the point; they aren't buying them voluntarily. Their poverty coerces them into some scheme for escape, no matter how unlikely it is to succeed."

Gordon thought of a dozen responses to that but knew none would satisfy her.

"Lotteries are taxes on people who are bad at math," he said.

"Lotteries are scams on the proletariat," she countered, shutting down her computer and getting her purse. "I'm too hungry to argue; let's go."

At the restaurant called "Los Dos Caballos," they ate chicken, plantains, rice, and beans, while a scratchy recording of Xavier Cugat played in the background. Gordon suddenly began coughing as he had mistaken a chili pepper for a sun-dried tomato. Zera called for the waiter in Spanish, and he brought Gordon a glass of ice water.

When desserts and coffee were served, Zera looked at him with a studied gaze and asked, "So why do you want to be a dusty, musty old professor?"

He sighed and talked about the classics and Father Kottmeyer, but in the end said he was now reconsidering the whole thing.

"I've never known what I wanted to be; teaching came by default. I had always done well in school, especially with languages, and came to the conclusion it was the only thing I could succeed at." He took a breath and said softly, "I know I can be a dork sometimes about most practical matters."

"So what would you do if not something academic?"

"I'm not sure, and even if I wanted to stay in graduate school, stealing antiquities pretty much eliminates you from classical studies."

"Sort of like pharmacists selling crack out the back door, or IRS agents cheating on their taxes," she said with a giggle. Zera was a bit tipsy now from drinking most of the bottle of Pinot Grigio but for the half glass Gordon had. She became jovial and gave herself over to flirting, inviting body language, and even coquettish asides, something Gordon knew her more sober, doctrinaire side would have disapproved of had it been in control.

Gordon walked her home and she invited him in.

"Do you play games?" she asked.

Gordon's mind raced as it turned to the possibilities of erotic teasing, cross-dressing, or the use of edible materials in bed, all of which he had read about but had never tried personally.

"Scrabble, maybe?" she said, and he felt then that he had lived in New York too long as he was surprised when something wasn't jaded.

She brought out the board and letter tiles. They began the game and she quickly racked up some points, followed by a triple word score, as he tried hopelessly to make a word from two Ms, two Ws, and a D.

On her shelf Gordon noticed Copleston's *History of Philosophy*, and she brought out a tin which contained some of Granny Gardner's cookies, his favorite brand. For a few hours, he forgot his troubles and felt he was in the best place on earth. He ate cookies while she talked about epistemology and the food in North Africa, Marxism, Surrealism, collective farms, and getting booted out of a kibbutz for not obeying rules. Her brown eyes danced with a primal enthusiasm for ideas. She was, Gordon thought, the most brilliant woman he had ever met.

When she put down her last tile on the Scrabble board, they added the score sheet. She had beaten him mercilessly in three straight games with words like "xebec" and "zygote" running off one another. She changed the names on the sheet from "Zera" and "Gordon" to "Einstein" and "Stallone".

"Hah; you are my prisoner now," she cackled, getting up from the cushion she sat on to pour herself more wine.

When she returned to the front room, she sat next to him on the couch, close enough to be touching elbows. He put his arm over her shoulder, but this seemed to snap her back to sobriety.

"Gordon, I think we should just be friends and leave sex in the bottle unopened. It would never work and you've got enough on your plate."

"I'll take that as a no for now, but don't expect me to give up so easily."

She walked him to the door and kissed him on the cheek. He took the train uptown while thinking of ways to dissuade her from her resistance, but he had no sound reasons, only the pressing demands of his own heart.

He called her on Monday, but she said she was on her way to her therapist.

"I didn't know you were in therapy."

"Why on earth would you think I wasn't?" she said.

There was a silence and he said, "What do you expect to get from therapy?"

"My only goal is to live honestly," she answered.

"I think that's a worthy one."

"Yes, but getting there is a journey, and half the time I try to piss my shrink off to get a reaction: like last week when I observed to him that 'therapist' can be broken down into 'the rapist'".

"What did he say to that?"

"That I wasn't the first to make that joke, and that is one of my problems; that I'm so egotistical that I imagine whatever I say has never been said before."

"Well, you have me convinced most of the time," Gordon told her.

"So if I can find a few hundred more like you, I have a cult."

Zera said she was going to Washington to do some interviews and would be back in a week. Gordon moped for a few days and then immersed himself in making notes on Herodotus since he was barred from the Penniman. It made him feel better to read something he liked, and he decided the police really didn't consider him a suspect. If they did, something would have happened by now. They try to scare people into confessing, he reasoned, and when he didn't, they moved on to other avenues. Another few days passed and then the weekend, making him feel that Sabatini had certainly focused on other suspects, but at three o'clock on Monday his doorbell rang, surprisingly since he had few visitors. He thought perhaps it was Zera, now disposed to considering his romantic overtures.

"Who is it?" he called through the intercom.

"Mmfg bratz bini," the voice answered through the ancient box.

He buzzed the entry button and went to the hallway, knowing he would have enough time to duck into his flat if it was an intruder. He looked over the stairwell railings to see Detective Sabatini, another man in a suit, and two uniformed police officers ascending to his landing.

"Police," Sabatini said as he reached the landing and saw Gordon. "We have a search warrant for your apartment, Bauer."

Gordon allowed them to enter, and they systematically took apart every drawer, shelf, and box, heaping clothes on the bed, books onto the floor, and papers everywhere. He stood there in silence watching them. As one went into the bathroom to search there, Sabatini gruffly said to Gordon; "I want to know why you were at the Stanopoulos Galleries."

"I was trying to find out what an amphora like the one stolen would sell for," Gordon said, immediately realizing how incriminating that sounded.

"Interesting," Sabatini said. "Thinking about selling one?"

"No, I was working to exonerate myself by trying to imagine who might have actually stolen it."

"Please, I was born at night, but I wasn't born last night."

"I didn't steal anything," Gordon said in protest.

"That isn't how I have it figured. First, the vase is discovered missing moments after you fled the hall, while the day before, this mysterious black kid comes to visit you. Now you are trying to find a way to fence it. I figure you got yourself involved with some street hustler with a coke problem and found the cost of keeping a boy like that was to steal from the museum. I'd say you had motive and opportunity."

"I'm not keeping a boy," Gordon said.

"Okay, renting, then," the other detective said with a laugh.

"Hey, being gay isn't a crime," Sabatini said, "but larceny is. Maybe that Illinois upbringing fell by the wayside once you got to New York, came out of the closet, and discovered you needed money to pay to keep him around."

"That's not it at all," Gordon remonstrated.

"Hey, you're into Greek things," the other detective said. "We all know what went on with those guys and their boyfriends." He laughed hysterically as Gordon's face grew redder and he felt tears welling up in his eyes.

"Are you sure you don't want to confess?' Sabatini said. "It will go easier on you if you just tell us now."

"I didn't steal it," Gordon said.

Sabatini took a breath and removed an envelope from his pocket.

"Our search warrant also covered your desk at the Penniman. We went there before coming here, and taped to the back of one of your desk drawers was this envelope."

Sabatini opened the envelope and showed Gordon a package of hundred dollar bills.

"I've never seen that," Gordon said in shock.

"This note was with the bills," Sabatini said and showed Gordon a typewritten note which read:

"You'll get the rest of your split when it has been sold."

"Bingo," Sabatini said. "Your fence has made the case for us. You're under arrest for the theft of the Columbia am-fow-ra."

Gordon couldn't find his voice for a moment, trying to decide if they had planted the envelope, or if someone else trying to shift the blame to him had done so.

"I'm being framed, "Gordon said.

"Just as an aside," Sabatini said, "You're a pretty dumb thief. If the vase is worth fifty thousand or more and you only got three…." He snorted and waved to the two uniformed officers who handcuffed Gordon and led him down the four flights of steps.

"I'm innocent," Gordon said as he stood on the sidewalk waiting for one of the officers to open the back door of the cruiser.

He looked and saw Alma Wyatt talking with Frank Kelley. They stopped their conversation and stared at Gordon in handcuffs but said nothing, their faces registering disbelief.

"It is my duty to inform you of your constitutional rights," Sabatini began. "You have the right to remain silent…"

The rest Gordon only half heard. A waterfall in his head drowned out the rest of the Miranda warning.

Once back at the precinct house they fingerprinted and photographed him. It was bad television come to life, Gordon thought. They put him in a small cell and shortly thereafter allowed him to make a telephone call. He dialed Zera and told her what had happened. She said she would call Harvey and get him released. Gordon sat in the interrogation room sobbing. How could he tell his parents about this? Who would believe him?

"Do you want to confess, kid? Maybe give us the name of your boyfriend and the fence? We can keep the gay part out of the courtroom proceedings if that's what's worrying you," Sabatini said.

"I didn't do it," he sobbed.

"Yeah, yeah. You think you're tough, but you're not tough enough for prison. Work with us and if the vase can be recovered, maybe you can get straight probation if this is a first offense."

"Straight probation" the other detective laughed. "Maybe gay probation instead. If your boyfriend cops a plea, you can ride off into the sunset together."

"Think about it," Sabatini said.

Gordon wept quietly although he hated himself for doing it. Once a wimp, always a wimp, he thought.

"Boo-hoo, boo-hoo," the other detective said as he left the room.

The sound of being mocked as he sat there quivering and crying made him realize why women did not fall madly in love with him, why clerks did not wait on him first even when he was first in line, and why he was often overlooked at parties. He was a weak-kneed sissy, he told himself, a wuss of world-class proportions, a miserable muck of warm jelly.

And then Gordon found himself getting angry, very angry. Angry for the snubs from pretty girls, the frogs put down his back, for always being the one chosen to play right field or mind the baseball bats. His tears suddenly dried, and it dawned on him that the envelope of money, the story of the young black man, the fact that his visit to Stanopoulos was known, all appeared as hinges to the same conclusion: that someone had put all the arrows in place that pointed to Gordon, someone able to construct a perfect storm of opportunity to frame him for the crime. Who, he did not know, but as inescapable as June being followed by July, it was a conspiracy.

He sat up in his chair, his head held high, and looked Sabatini directly in the eyes.

"I did not do this. I am being set up by the person who did, and if you can't find this son of a bitch, I'm going to."

Sabatini shrugged, put his unlit cigar in his mouth, looked at the no-smoking sign, and then lit it anyway.

"We're going to start all over again from the beginning," he said. "But if you're innocent, I'm the effing King of Romania."

VII

"Can I use my student loan money to post bail?"

HARVEY AND ZERA SHOWED UP an hour later and were told Gordon would be transported to the courthouse for a bail hearing. When a magistrate set bail at $25,000, Harvey stayed at the courthouse while Zera left and came back with a cashier's check for the full amount.

"I can't let you do this," Gordon protested.

"I didn't; Darwin's friend Robertson posted bail; he was so convinced of your sincerity that he is sure you weren't a thief."

"But…," Gordon said without finishing his thought.

"But I cannot possibly crack the case and get my story with you in the slammer. End of discussion. Let's get out of here; we have work to do."

On the courthouse steps, Harvey advised them against playing detective on their own.

"I can hire an investigator if we need one. Let's see what the district attorney presents as his case first. This money found at your desk sounds bogus, and it does seem as if someone inside the museum is trying to get you to take the fall."

"They would appear to have succeeded," Gordon said ruefully.

Zera and Gordon went uptown to his flat and had iced tea at his kitchen table while Zera made a chart of which direction their actions should take. She took a large paper bag stuffed beside the refrigerator and the table and cut it open, spread it on the table, and together they drew a map of the Penniman and surrounding buildings. She began drawing lines, arrows, and dashes to show means of access and escape for anyone who had been in the room where it was kept.

Zera made three columns on the back of the bag, titling them "Ideological Perpetrators", "Art Thieves" and "Common Criminals". Zera put in parentheses "Oppressed Minorities" next to the last and Gordon groaned.

"You never give it a rest, do you?" he said. "It's always societal, never individual."

"Are you the reincarnation of Margaret Thatcher?" she said, laughing a little.

"I just think in the end people choose to act as they act."

"I still have a lot of work to do with you," Zera sighed. "So let's get you out of this jam."

The radio talk shows and papers had continued to cover the amphora story and Fontana's theory, so Gordon and Zera decided to search online and find everyone who weighed in on the amphora and its significance.

"You don't have Wi-Fi?" she said incredulously as she waited for a connection on her tablet.

"Classicists don't need Wi-Fi," he retorted.

They decided that art thieves would not be people they knew, and went to the common criminal category, deciding to canvass the Morningside Heights, but first having one more look at Mandeville Hall and its surroundings.

"Someone might be bribed or persuaded to give us something they noticed that night," Zera said. "All police say their CIs are the most important resource."

"CIs?" Gordon said quizzically.

"Confidential informants. Jeez, Louise; don't you ever watch any of the cop shows?"

"I usually just watch PBS," he said dismissively.

"So, what about all those British detective shows on that channel?"

"Not really, "Gordon said.

"And no tablet, Wi-Fi, or a freaking clue how the real world works. Gordon; you can't spend your life in 480 BC at Thermopylae!"

Gordon winced because up until then, that was exactly where he wanted to spend his life. He washed his hands to get rid of the black fingerprint ink, scrubbing each finger diligently. He imagined what would happen if he went to prison; he had seen all those old black-and-white films of prison life where someone in the laundry got stabbed with an improvised knife made in the metal shop. He imagined a burly weightlifter as a cellmate who would call him "the new chicken" and offer him protection in return for unspeakable acts.

"Are you going to tell your parents?' Zera called to him from the kitchen.

"God, no," Gordon replied. "Could you call yours and say you had been arrested?"

"Actually I have: twice. Once as a teenager for drunk and disorderly conduct, although it was my boyfriend who was drunk, I was only disorderly. The second time was when I was arrested outside the Pentagon, but my parents were lefty when they were young, so they were proud of me that time."

"Well, mine wouldn't be. If I go to prison, I will have to invent some story about joining the Peace Corps."

The next morning at eight they met at the Broadway Gate of Columbia, and Zera went to find the custodians and office workers who were going about their tasks in Mandeville Hall. Gordon, since he was barred from the building, walked around the campus to see what he or the police might have missed about the general layout. University buildings had a quiet dignity to them that intimated life was about study and contemplation. To have nothing unusual happening was considered the stability needed for scholarship. He looked about at the staidness of the campus and wondered if a contemplative life was really a desirable goal. For some it was an escape. He thought of Hector Lampurdy, the star of the department, a Latinist who would be receiving his PhD the following year. Hector was one of the few people more detached from daily life than Gordon. He was pale, orderly, quiet, and effortlessly pounded out translations of odes and epics like deli men slice bologna, as well as arcane essays peppered with terms like "Discourse" and "Appropriation". He had mastered the game well, Gordon thought, but he wasn't alive. A question put to Hector was always pondered, mulled, and digested before a long, careful answer was given. Gordon couldn't think of any occasion when Hector became emotional over a subject, sprang to his feet, and said the first thing that leaped into his mind. No to that, Gordon thought, if the price of an academic career was spending life in an intense, guarded state so as never to utter a silly word.

His love of the ancient authors was partly excitement over discoveries; who would have thought Xenophon's *Anabasis* could trump Caesar's *Gallic Wars,* or that Catullus properly translated could be so smutty? The notion that Homer actually could have been a blind poet capable of composing lines by the thousands was astonishing, and the beauty of Latin odes stirring. The Greek tragedies could all be imagined so clearly when he did the translations, even to the chants of the choruses. Marcus Aurelius was a genius, and the Socratic dialogues drove him to consider eternal themes in philosophy. Even satires and jokes were novel, thinking that ancient man also saw the ironies and hypocrisies of life. Modern man, Gordon often said, thought he invented everything in the same way that teenagers imagined they had invented sex.

But this long train of thoughts about the classics didn't now seem to resolve issues with his own life. To be inspired and pleased by literature didn't equate to earning a living from it. Perhaps thinking that because he had done well in certain subjects, he should use them for a livelihood was flawed thinking. To be educated was a goal in itself, but the way one earned a living was not synonymous with education alone. Man had to act, take stands, and move events rather than passively wait for them to occur; if there was any lesson the ancient heroes taught, wasn't it that?

Gordon walked about the campus thinking more about his issues with academic life than in mystery solving, and when he reconnected with Zera two hours later, he had little of use to say. They walked back to his apartment and when they got to the front door they saw an ambulance pull up and EMTs take a stretcher and bring it up the stairs. Frank Kelley was there and looked agitated.

"It's Alma," he said to Gordon. "She wasn't feeling well and had chest pains, so I called 911."

Gordon and Zera waited for Alma to be taken out. He squeezed her hand and said he would do what he could to help. She smiled and disappeared into the ambulance. Frank said he would call her daughter and let her know.

The heat of midsummer was rising even though it was not yet noon. His brick building would become an oven by late in the day, and across the street, a work crew was digging a hole on the other side of Amsterdam Avenue where a water pipe had burst. They sweated and dug, their torsos glistening with moisture. The jackhammer pounded away relentlessly, and Zera suggested they go to her place since she had an air conditioner.

They took the train downtown and then walked to her flat on West 51st. Once there she ordered some Thai take-out and they sat down to consider their strategies.

"We'll start with your common thief theory," Zera began. She drew lines in pencil on her map. "He came in for what reason? To use the toilets, to raid the vending machine, because he had been a classics student before becoming homeless and knew about the amphora lecture?"

Gordon grimaced, knowing this theory had holes from the start.

"Tomorrow we work the neighborhood to see if any of the downtrodden know anything, but I think it had to be a random chance for a thief to just wander in."

They plotted ways to obtain the trust of people on the edges of society, and the next day, armed with self-confidence if not knowledge of the streets, they started at Best Buzz and soon found a man panhandling for change in front of the store. He was incoherent, and so they walked north, looking at every street corner or doorstep for down-at-the-heels characters. At Morningside Park, they saw a few men sharing a whisky bottle from a brown paper bag and approached them.

Zera walked up to them and smiled. "Hey, how's it going?"

"Hey yourself," one answered with a clip of sarcasm in his voice.

Zera took out her cigarettes and struck her fingers on the bottom to produce a few. She offered one to each of them and gave them a light. Their hands were dirty and rough as they held the cigarettes to the flame.

"My friend and I are trying to find something that's lost," she began.

The three drinkers looked at her apprehensively.

"It was a vase about this big," Zera said, gesturing with her hands.

There was silence and finally one man said, "How did you lose it?"

"That's a long story, but there's a reward if it's found."

"How much?" one of the men asked.

"A thousand dollars," Zera said.

One whistled, and the others suddenly looked more interested.

Just then a disheveled woman in a stained blue windbreaker came up to them.

"Hey, boys," she said.

"Hey, Mary," one answered.

"Got a smoke?"

Zera produced another cigarette for the woman who looked

sixty, but was likely no more than forty-five. Her hair was dirty and her shoes nearly worn through. When she took the first drag of the cigarette, she burst into a fit of coughing.

"Mary, do you know anything about a stolen vase that might have turned up somewhere near here?" Zera asked.

"I didn't steal anything," she protested reflexively. She waved the cigarette like a wand.

"It was large and had paintings on it."

She shook her head.

"If you want anything from her, you'll have to give her drinking money," one of the men said. "They call her 'Bushmills Mary' 'cuz she drinks the Irish stuff."

Zera wrestled with giving alcoholics money for liquor, but peeled a five-dollar bill off a roll, then one for all the others.

"If you hear of anything, call this number," she said, pulling out one of her business cards that gave her number at the paper.

They looked at the card in a perplexed way but said they would ask around. The four shuffled off in the direction of a liquor store.

"I shouldn't have done that," Zera said.

"They can't drink all the time," Gordon said. "Sooner or later they will have to buy a hamburger."

Bushmills Mary turned back and waved. "The people in the spaceship might have taken it; they take all kinds of stuff that goes missing around here," she said.

They walked away leaving Zera and Gordon to stare at one another, Gordon acknowledging that even if it were true that a street thief was the culprit, it would be nearly impossible to find out given the reliability of likely informants like Mary.

"I think we have to move on to the premise that this was a crime of ideology," she said. "It's the problem of the drunk and the street lamp."

"What's that?"

"You never heard that bit of wisdom? It is about a drunk who loses his car keys and starts looking under the street lamp. Someone asks him why he is limiting his search and he reasons, even though drunk, that if they are under the street lamp he will see them, and if they are somewhere else, he won't, so he might as well look where he has a chance of finding them. It is kind of logic on its ear, but it makes sense."

"So what next?"

"Columbia's insurance company. I am sure the university has already filed a claim. Harvey can get a court order if they aren't willing to give up any information. They surely investigate such things before paying out; they may have a lead the police haven't gotten to yet."

Zera called Harvey on her cell phone and explained what they wanted. In a few hours, after they had absorbed sunshine and torti-llas from a sidewalk table at a Mexican place at Broadway and 104th, Harvey called back and said they should meet at his office at ten the next morning. He would go with them to the insurance company in the hope that something useful would be revealed.

Zera went home, and Gordon went to the Lenox Hill Hospital to see Alma, who was resting comfortably. Happily, it was not a heart attack, but severe indigestion due to a likely ulcer in the esophagus. She had some other issues and they were doing some more tests but she would soon be sent home. He told her about the trouble with the police but said he would be exonerated. She smiled and held his hand before drifting off to sleep.

On the way back to his building, a summer darkness overtook the city. Huge billowing clouds came in from New Jersey, and the air felt heavier than a lump of wet feathers. The smell of summer rain when it began to fall made Gordon feel strangely happy. Things from the sensory world, he realized, had come to lose their impact as his life had become journeys from classroom to library. People in Manhattan were so busy with their daily activities that it seemed irrelevant whether it was winter or summer. Gordon thought of flowers as they bloomed and the earth under his feet that turned to mud when it rained. Just then bolts of lightning and claps of thunder brought him out of his reverie. The deluge began at four o'clock and the rain scoured the pavements, dissolving the images he could see from his window. Only a few yellow slickered people and the red river of tail lights trying to exit Manhattan in rush hour now moving at a snail's pace were discernible. In an hour the rain stopped and the sun began shining through the haze. Gordon smiled to think the pot of gold at the end of the rainbow now forming was probably in Newark.

The next morning Gordon was up early and met Zera at Harvey's office. They walked from there to the insurance company's office near Grand Central Station. Harvey had learned that Columbia had filed a claim, and the vice president in charge had agreed to see them. The July day was warm and pleasant as they walked. The flavored ice vendors had set up their carts, and it was to be at least another day before the heat broke. Gordon realized then that the notion of hell as a flammable place made perfect sense. As they approached the sixty-story skyscraper, they read the name carved in granite on a frieze at the second-floor level: "American Guaranty Insurance

Company." On a stone shield below was the legend "Stability Since 1844."

"Stability, my ass," Harvey muttered. "Their bond rating dropped after they announced writing off half a billion dollars in bad investments. But don't worry; they're only laying off a thousand people to make it up. The CEO's yacht will be safe."

They entered the lobby and checked in at the security desk. They were given plastic visitor badges and directed to the elevator bank and the thirty-fifth floor. Gordon felt his ears pop as they rapidly ascended in the cherry-paneled and mirrored compartment with a tiny television reminding them the stock market was falling and the oceans rising. A soft ding announced their arrival and the door opened. Cool air hit their faces and the deep carpeting swallowed their footfalls as they went to the reception desk.

"We're here to see Alana Savalescu," Harvey said with confidence in his voice, handing the receptionist his card.

"One moment please," the receptionist replied. She dialed a number and spoke through the tiny microphone attached to her headset.

"Mr. Knippelman is here."

She told them to be seated, and a few minutes later a mid-thirtyish woman in a blue jacket and skirt with a starched white blouse, scarf, and expensive gold pin came out to greet them.

"I'm Alana Savalescu," she said and shook hands with the three of them, then led them down a long hallway with nautical prints hung along the wall.

They followed her into an office with a fine view of the East Side. Her office had traditional mahogany furniture, a coffee table with issues of *Risk Management Today* magazine, and a framed print of the

Eiffel Tower. The credenza behind her desk had the usual assortment of knick-knacks; a small world globe, a picture of a four-year-old boy who no doubt spent more time with a nanny than Alana, some awards, and a small brass monkey whose significance Gordon could only guess at. The quiet in the office was unearthly, broken only by the low murmur of the air conditioning.

Harvey opened his briefcase and spread some photocopies of the news stories on her desk, as well as some information he had put together on Gordon and his responsibilities at the Penniman.

"I want to open by saying my client is an innocent man and has fully cooperated with the police investigation," Harvey began.

"Which investigation now considers Mr. Bauer the prime target, I understand, "Alana Savalescu said coolly.

"Only because they aren't looking in the right direction," Zera chimed in.

"And you would be…?"

"I'm an investigative journalist covering the story, Zera said, pounding her finger on one of the articles spread before Alana that was from the *Liberator* with Zera's byline.

"Well, we've paid no claim yet and haven't given up on the idea that the vase is recoverable."

"Let me ask you a few questions, then," Harvey said in a conciliatory tone, and he went on to inquire how companies decide to pay claims, what they do to recover property, and how difficult it might be for someone to sell an object like the Black Amphora.

"The last question is our best friend," she said. "There are websites and databases that track stolen art works. The FBI and Interpol share information and reputable dealers report attempts to sell stolen items. That leaves people who steal to order for private collectors who don't care that they can never show them, or dishonest dealers who will, for a slice of the pie, deal in stolen art."

Gordon made mental notes while Harvey continued his questions.

"There is another scenario that sometimes occurs," she said quietly, as if betraying a trade secret. "The thief offers the object back to its owner."

"For ransom, I assume," Harvey said.

"Exactly. We don't encourage this, but sometimes owners would rather have the object than the insurance money. When they are too willing to take the insurance money, we worry about fraud."

"We feel it was either a common criminal, or someone inside Columbia who knew the value, how to steal it, and believed he could fence it," Harvey said.

Gordon was crestfallen then as he realized the definition fit him, which was why the police were going down the same road.

"But I have a third theory," Zera interjected. "If someone wanted to make Fontana's postulate on the Afrocentric origins of Greek civilization unprovable, one way would be to make the amphora disappear before it could be examined further."

Alana Savalescu folded her hands in front of her on the desk. "I couldn't speculate, only to say that if Mr. Bauer has any information the police don't have, he should be forthcoming with it."

Gordon again protested his innocence, but with nothing left to discuss, they shook hands and left.

Harvey went back to his office, while Gordon and Zera walked in silence.

"If it's in a private collection by now, we'll never know," Gordon said, "and I'll be two to five years upstate to think about what I will be doing afterward, maybe longer if a jury decided Longstreet's death was precipitated by a robbery. That's how much time Harvey said I would serve if convicted."

"Don't be so gloomy, Gus. We still have leads to work on."

She persuaded him to accompany her back to the newspaper office on Twelfth Street, and Gordon followed her up the stairs of an old building to the second floor where half a dozen desks lay nearly buried in paper. It was a rabbit's warren of files, boxes, coffee cups, old issues of *The Liberator,* and the ringing of phones.

"Come with me and I'll introduce you to the boss," Zera said.

They walked into a back office with a glass partition, and a man of about forty-five with wiry, undisciplined hair and a wan blue Oxford shirt sat banging away on a keyboard.

"Hey, chief; meet the subject of the Columbia amphora story."

Darwin got up and shook Gordon's hand.

"Zera tells me you're innocent and she's going to prove it."

"I hope so," Gordon said.

Just then a tall woman with a heap of strawberry blonde hair pushed to the top of her head entered the room.

"Oh, Mali, this is Gordon Bauer."

The woman extended her hand and Gordon wondered, as he stared into her Caucasian face with Hibernian pug nose and freckles, how she had been named for an African country.

"I have to ask about your name," Gordon began. "Were your parents in the Peace Corps?"

She stared at him as if he had sprouted antlers.

"Did someone tell you they were?"

"No, it's just your name: 'Mali'"?

"Mali?" she said, looking at Zera for the joke. "My name is Molly Finnegan."

Just then it became apparent to the three of them that Zera's New York accent had been the cause of the misconception. They laughed and agreed that someone from Illinois would hear it exactly as he had.

Zera went to her desk to answer e-mail while Gordon flipped through an almanac he took from a bookshelf near the window. He looked at a list of countries, examining their flags and vital statistics, wondering as he did which of them may not have extradition treaties with the United States.

When Zera was done, they left the newspaper and walked to the subway.

"Okay; meet me at the Best Buzz up by you at nine o'clock tomorrow morning and prepare to radicalize yourself. Why wouldn't an opponent of Fontana's theory take the amphora? Honor? Decency? Do you think professors have higher standards than people on the street? There are some people we are going to corner. Have a good breakfast; we have work to do. I don't want you going off to prison; you amuse me too much!"

Gordon went to his uptown train and thought that was the sweetest thing anyone in New York had said to him.

VIII

"I would make them all learn English,
and then I would let the clever ones learn
Latin as a reward, and Greek as a treat."

— WINSTON CHURCHILL

"ALL RIGHT; WE'VE GOT LOTS of ground to cover, so drink up," Zera said, handing Gordon a coffee as he walked in the door of Best Buzz the next morning. "I got you a mocha latte, and I have the Sulawesi dark roast. Unless you'd rather switch?"

"Latte is fine; I doubt they serve them in the New York State corrections system."

"Sit," Zera said, and they took a table where she opened a window on her tablet and clicked on photographs downloaded from the internet. "I have biographical information here on the main opponents who wrote op-ed pieces in *The New York Times* or appeared as guests on radio or television weighing in on the matter."

Clicking on one she said, "Here's John Parker Doody, for starters. He teaches history at NYU and has written a series of fulminating articles about the decline of Western civilization and the negative effects of multi-culturalism."

The picture showed a tall, gawky man, all chin and nose.

"He doesn't look like a thief," Gordon said.

Zera fumed. "That is your mindset. Does a thief look more black or just more lower class?"

Gordon was ready to answer, but she put her head down and continued to read more names.

"Margaret Harris; do you know her?"

"She's a post-doc fellow in classics at Columbia."

"Which one is her in this picture?"

Gordon looked at a digital photo from the night of the lecture. The traditionalists marching with the poster board drawing of the Parthenon were led by Margaret, a short, obese woman with straight black hair just over her ears, blue rimmed glasses, and a scowl.

"That's her, "Gordon said. "Right up front."

"She was apparently the main organizer of the demonstration and has written letters and spoken in public debunking Afrocentrism."

"I thought she was just strange."

"And lastly there is Humphrey Gaskins, the syndicated columnist, who has a daily radio show and is known for his ridicule of affirmative action, environmentalism, and women," Zera said. She pulled up several of his columns including a recent one on the Black Amphora. Another one correlated the decline in reading scores to the teaching of black history, teenage pregnancy to rock and roll, and in a long, thundering jeremiad, illegal immigration to offering food stamps.

"I will admit to being somewhat traditional in my views, but even by my Illinois standards, Humphrey Gaskins qualifies as a nut case."

"Halleluiah," Zera said, taking a cigarette from her purse. "I'm making some headway with you." She put the cigarette away and sighed. "I'm trying, really trying."

Gordon looked the screen where Zera had cut and pasted the pictures of the three individuals. "Where do we start?" he said.

"I think we should call on all of them. Who knows, one might get edgy and spill the beans."

They looked up the addresses of the three. Doody and Harris were listed, while Gaskins was not.

He writes out of the offices of the *New York Examiner*," Zera said. "We can cold call him there."

They took a cab to the village and went to Doody's apartment first. It was Saturday and they chanced he would be home. The building was modest and they walked up the steps and rang the bell. After two rings a man opened the door.

"The intercom doesn't work; are you from the air conditioning repair?"

"Not exactly," Zera said, wedging her foot in the door. "I'm with the *Twelfth Street Liberator,* and we'd like to talk with you about the Columbia amphora."

He looked at her with disdain. "That claptrap Marxist rag?"

"I'm only trying to be objective. I thought the *Times* could have given you more space for that op-ed piece you wrote," she said, playing the flattery card.

"You think?" he said, more amiable now. "Yes, a short column was barely enough to scratch the surface. Come in," he said, "but if you distort my words, I'll sue."

"I will be happy to let you see any comments I attribute to you before we go to press," Zera said, although she knew if she had good copy, Darwin would want to run it immediately.

"Who is your friend; Leon Trotsky's grandson?" Doody said, looking at a newly sprouted mustache and goatee Gordon had begun on a whim a few days earlier.

"No, he's my interpreter. He studies classics at Columbia, and if it's any consolation, he's a hopeless Hellenist."

The professor took them to his front room and sat them down on an overstuffed couch. Books lined every wall while papers, journals, and files were stuffed in and around every piece of furniture.

Zera took out her tablet and began quietly. "Coming out of the box we're trying to see if this vase is actually important to proving or disproving any links between Greek civilization and Africa."

Doody frowned as he sat down in a chair, first moving books off the seat, the arms, and the ottoman.

"I suppose if you believe such a silly thing in the first place, a vase is as good as anything to offer as proof. The theory fails for reasons other than that; I will lend you a book that debunks the whole thing."

He got up and walked to a book case, stepping around a pile of books, pushing aside a box of books, and eventually standing on three books to reach what he wanted. Here was a man, Gordon thought, whose very existence was not only measured in books, but was being devoured by them. Zera took the volume when he handed it to her, but held it on her lap while she changed the subject.

"You were at the demonstration the night of Dr. Fontana's lecture; did you see anything suspicious?"

"I didn't steal the damned thing or know who did, if that's what you are searching for. I told the police everything I know."

"So you were interviewed by the police?" Zera said, her ears almost visibly twitching.

"I think they questioned everybody standing about. I went on a lark because I love tweaking the noses of people like Fontana and all their political correctness."

"Do you think someone who opposes the 'Black Athena' theory could or would have stolen it as a way of stopping the debate?" Zera asked.

"No," Doody replied. "I mean anything is possible, but if you, we, me, anyone believed the theory was disprovable, why would we take it? Maybe someone promoting the theory who had doubt that it could be proven took it. Why do you think one ideological group is dishonest and the other pure and disinterested?"

"That's what I keep telling her," Gordon chimed in.

Zera fumed. "In my experience people with the power are the ones more likely to be dishonest to hold onto that power rather than those who seek to undermine the status quo."

Doody stared at her. "Then I think you are rather a naïve young lady; what on earth does ideology have to do with honesty? Butchers and despots exist on the right and the left. Where on earth did you study history? Some Bolshevik summer camp?"

Zera was ready to unload, but Gordon gripped her by the elbow.

"Well, thanks for seeing us," Gordon said and drew himself and Zera to their feet to leave.

"Read that book," Doody said as he showed them out. "But get it back to me. You know what Mark Twain said about lending books? He said he never did it because people never brought them back. He knew because his whole library was composed of other people's books."

On the sidewalk Gordon shrugged. "What do you think?"

"That he is a typical conservative apologist."

"Did you go to Bolshevik summer camp?" Gordon asked.

"I went to youth camps for progressive thinking in Vermont," she snapped.

"I was joking, and Doody was as well."

She made a noise half between a growl and a sigh.

"When you have your revolution, I think you need to have a ministry for humor," he said.

Zera lit a cigarette and puffed it furiously.

"It is interesting that Sabatini questioned him. It means the police themselves might also be wondering if it was stolen for reasons other than money," she said. "Margaret Harris is next; do you know her well enough to call her?"

"Barely, but let's do it anyway," Gordon said, surprised at his newfound courage.

He called on Zera's cell, and Margaret vaguely knew who he was from departmental events. She said she was home if they wanted to come by.

They took the train to the Upper West Side and went to her apartment on West 115th. She buzzed them in and they walked up three flights. Looking through the security peephole, Margaret finally unlocked the two locks, unchained the door, and removed the steel rod that was anchored to the floor to prevent the door from being pushed open.

"I heard they arrested a student; I didn't know it was you," she said.

"He didn't do it," Zera quickly added.

"May we ask you some questions?" Gordon said.

Margaret pointed to a weathered rust-colored couch that sat on a matching Bokhara rug and whose geometries were dizzying. The couch was ragged, having been clawed nearly to oblivion by a black cat who napped on a pile of papers in the corner. Gordon asked the same questions they asked Doody and she answered them, staring through thick lenses which magnified her eyes. Her limp hair, a tent dress, and a terrible case of eczema on her hands made her the least attractive woman Gordon had ever laid eyes on. She offered them tea and spilled the water, smashed a cup, and then couldn't find teabags.

"What's all the noise?" a man's voice with an English accent called out.

Zera and Gordon looked to the hallway and saw a young man in a bathrobe. He had long, dark hair and a sallow, sunken visage that conspired to make him look handsome in a rugged, unkempt way.

"I'm just making tea for these people, Clive; go back to bed."

"Do be a little quieter, love, eh?" he said, shuffling back to the bedroom.

"That's my boyfriend," Margaret giggled. "He plays in a band and has to sleep days."

Gordon thought to himself that if Margaret Harris could find a mate in New York, but he couldn't, there was something wrong with either the universe or himself. Zera asked some more questions about the traditionalists, and it was clear they were not an organized movement, but merely people whose only unifying principle was a general dissatisfaction with the modern world. Gordon and Zera got up to leave, sharing an unspoken agreement that none of this shed any light on the missing amphora. Margaret showed them out, but not before knocking over a coat stand, cutting her finger on the door lock, and scattering adhesive bandages over the floor attempting to peel one free from the backing and apply it to the wound.

When she finally covered the finger with Zera's help, she saw them to the stairwell. A draft slammed her apartment door shut and Margaret exclaimed, "My keys are inside!" She went back to the door and banged on it until she woke up Clive again. Zera and Gordon walked downstairs to the street.

Zera said, "I have to admit she's not the type who would be stealing something to make a point."

"She's not the kind of person who COULD steal anything. She's so maladroit she would have broken the thing into five thousand pieces before getting it out of the building," Gordon replied.

Their last stop of the day was at the *New York Guardian* to find Humphrey Gaskins. They arrived at the building as the sun descended and caressed the Hudson River, casting its red rouge on the buildings.

They couldn't get past security, so they chose to wait near the door. A black limousine was parked nearby, and they assumed it was for Gaskins as his radio show began at nine o'clock and he was no doubt being whisked there. A short time later they saw a tall, heavyset man emerge from the elevator and pass down the hall to the door. He had silvery blond hair, blue eyes, and a cigar in hand. His pink skin and jovial expression were recognizable from the publicity photos they had. One might have thought him to bear a resemblance to Santa Claus but for his continual hectoring of the poor, immigrants, the disabled, and any government program designed to help them.

As he emerged, Zera walked up to him displaying her press pass. "Mr. Gaskins; a few questions?"

He seemed amused and flattered by the attention. Zera explained what their purpose was without betraying her own stand on the matter.

"Do you think the Columbia amphora that was stolen could in any way establish African roots for Greek civilization?"

Gaskins frowned and bluffed an answer. They could see he was over his head and had lost interest after it had given him a chance to rant about affirmative action. Zera asked whether any piece of classical scholarship might change his mind, and he responded by appeals to the flag, patriotism, and family values.

"We who are educated and the upholders of Western civilization and progress must defeat this hysterical nonsense that America and the West are not the heirs to the Greek ideal," he thundered.

Zera let him rumble on, touching on everything from prayer in school, the death penalty, and same-sex marriage. Finally, he said he had to leave as he was off to do his show. He shook hands with Zera and Gordon, and took two autographed color postcard pictures of himself from his pocket and gave them to them.

As the limousine sped off, Gordon asked Zera, "Does he seem suspicious?"

"The only thing I suspect him of being is drunk on his own vanity. I don't think the man actually believes anything he says; these issues are just vehicles for his ambition."

Zera sat down on a stone bench in the alley near the building. It was a small attempt at a park with a few potted plants. She looked down at her tablet and sighed.

"I feel as if I have let you down. I had my theories, but they aren't shaking anything loose that would help you."

He was surprised by this burst of doubt coming from a woman who was normally self-assured to the point of arrogance.

"Well, let's not have my farewell party yet."

They walked a while and considered what to have for dinner.

"Indian?" Zera offered. "Or vegetarian; there's a place near here."

"I suppose."

"Suppose is not an answer; vegetarian is too healthy for this point in time. I think right now you have a hankerin' for the Colonel's fare," she said, pointing to a Colonel Sanders chicken place across the street.

Gordon nodded and soon they were sitting at a Formica table with a bucket of fried chicken, a tub of mashed potatoes, and enough cole slaw to feed a regiment.

"This is good," Zera said, heaping some gravy on the potatoes.

"Didn't you just do an article on the high-fat content of fast food?" Gordon asked.

"I did, but that's not saying I don't like it."

When they were finished, Zera said she had to write, and Gordon, disappointed at not being asked to come back to her flat, took the train home. He fell into a dead sleep and woke the next day without ambition. It poured rain and thundered on and off while he watched re-runs of sitcoms from his boyhood, a spy film, a travelogue on Spain, and for a while even wrestling. He didn't raise the shades all day and felt himself increasingly antisocial. The world was giving him its final kick in the pants now, not being content with merely ignoring him.

The next day he went out, choosing to forget his troubles rather than dwell on them. He visited Alma in the hospital, and she said she was going to be discharged the next day.

"I'm not leaving this earth just yet," she said.

"That's great," Gordon said.

"Are you still in trouble with the police?" Alma asked.

"Yes, but I'm hoping for something to happen to clear me."

Alma sighed. "Son, nothing in this life just happens; you've got to make it happen."

She closed her eyes and went to sleep, and he reflected on that as he left the hospital. He walked to the East Side then to Madison, looking in shop windows at things he felt he would never be able to afford. He crossed over to head to Central Park, and at 75th and Madison he looked over to the Stanopoulos Galleries and considered how foolish it had been for him to go there. But how did Sabatini know, he asked himself? How did that visit where he never stated his name become circumstantial evidence against him? The police could have followed him for days and nights, but they didn't have that kind of manpower. Perhaps they made the rounds of galleries asking to look at videotapes of people who came in, but again it seemed unlikely.

Just before the traffic light changed, Gordon saw the gallery door open and Michael Fontana leave. In an instant, all of Gordon's suspicions came home to roost. Why was Fontana there? Could he have been doing what Gordon was suspected of doing: fencing the Black Amphora?

The story of the young black man, his visit to the gallery, the package of money that had been found in his desk at the Penniman; could all this be fruit from the same poisoned tree? His dislike of Fontana fueled the pleasure he felt in thinking Fontana was the thief. Gordon went home and wrote down every fact or suspicion, the times of everyone's comings and goings the night of the theft and before, and he realized that Fontana had the opportunity.

"What was the motive, though?" Zera asked when he phoned her to tell her what had happened.

"Notoriety, perhaps, by puffing up his little lecture into a drama."

"He has plenty of that already."

"True, but more is always more."

Zara was unconvinced, and later that night Gordon tried to think of a more tangible motive. Money seemed unlikely as full professors were not on food stamps.

"Unless he has expensive habits," Frank Kelley said when Gordon asked him for help the next day. The old man was listening to the Yankees game on the front stoop. "Gamblers, cocaine addicts, womanizers; they always need more money than they have."

"Have you ever known someone to steal something for what it represented, an idea perhaps?"

Kelley looked perplexed. "You're an educated man, I'm not, but maybe you're overthinking it. I was a cop for thirty-two years, and all the crime I saw pretty much came from what you read about in the Bible: greed, envy, lust, all that stuff. It never goes out of style." A roar came from the radio and Kelley snapped his fingers. "They got the run!"

Gordon knew that unless he was able to uncover something soon, the frame-up would stand. As an ex-convict he would have no life. He pictured himself living in rented rooms until he died, working menial jobs, and moving on when little children began pointing and adults talked about him behind his back. He would never marry nor have children, and with a long sigh he said, "Perhaps it's just as well to let the Bauer genes die out."

He went to the library the next morning, more to think than to read, and at noon he left to go back to his flat and a lunch of cheap cold cuts. As he crossed the campus to Amsterdam Avenue, he saw a yellow taxi pull up and an older man get out. The taxi waited as the man walked hurriedly, despite a limp, toward Mandeville Hall. Gordon recognized him as Dr. Rexford Runcie, one of the senior classics professors he had for the course in Roman historiographers. Runcie recognized Gordon and reached into his pocket, pulling out a large key ring and thrusting the keys into Gordon's hand.

"Gordon, dear boy," he began, huffing for breath. "You've saved me five minutes I don't have. I've got a plane to catch, and I don't want to lug these keys all over Pompeii while I'm studying inscriptions. Please bring these up to Miss Keefe, the departmental secretary, and have her hold them until I'm back next month."

"But…"Gordon started to say.

"Have to dash," Runcie said and made an about-face back to the taxi.

Gordon looked at the key ring and realized he likely now had access to every door and lock in Mandeville Hall. He looked around to see who might have witnessed the exchange, but only a few summer school students on the next pathway were anywhere near him. He thought for a moment, slipped the keys into his pocket, and headed for Amsterdam Avenue after Runcie's cab pulled away. It was the first time in his life he had disobeyed a teacher, broken a rule, or acted deceptively. Runcie lived in his own world and likely did not yet know about Gordon's arrest.

"I've caught a break," Gordon said when he called Zera to tell her what happened.

"Do you remember the story you told me of the drunk under

the lamplight; that he looked for his lost keys there because it was the only place he had enough light to see them?"

"Yes, and..."

"Well, I believe the answer will be found in Mandeville Hall if it's going to be found anywhere," he said. "For I am the drunk under the lamplight.

IX

"They Say the Naked Lady Has Something Up Her Sleeve"

T HE NEXT MORNING GORDON DISCLOSED his specific intentions. He and Zera sat in the Best Buzz watching the weary just jolted from their beds sugar their regulars, stir their lattes, and put straws into the towering, frozen mixed iced cappuccinos with abandon. With enough caffeine, Gordon thought, a man could conquer the world.

"You're going to break into Mandeville Hall to snoop around?" Zera said incredulously.

"Like a thief in the night."

"A black bag job, a Watergater," she said, her excitement level rising. "You do know what to bring in a burglar's bag, don't you?"

"I'm not looking to steal anything, but to get something back," he protested.

"I know, but I've read enough crime novels to know you have to be prepared."

They went back to Gordon's apartment and began to make a list.

"Dark clothing and a stocking cap, as well as several pairs of gloves, leather and latex, she began.

"Rope, flashlight, screwdriver, hammer, pliers," he added.

"WD-40, glue, a camera, notebook, pencil, and a thumb drive to download stuff from computers," she wrote.

"Coins for the photocopier, a towel to clean up, some food and water in case I get trapped somewhere for a while."

"We'll have to go to the store, and we have to limit ourselves to what can be carried in a gym bag."

When their list was done they went to five different stores, Zera producing a credit card for each purchase. Afterward, they went to a new Ethiopian restaurant called Addis Ababa, just off Broadway at 78th. They ate with their fingers and planned their mission.

On their way back to Columbia, walking on the east side of Broadway near the 116th Street gate, they saw a scruffy young man standing on the sidewalk next to dozens of books laid out for sale on a tablecloth, title sides up, with price markings in yellow stickies attached to each.

"Kant for four bucks," he said plaintively as they passed by.

"You can't what for four bucks?" Zera asked with a smile.

"I can't be a philosophy student all my life," the man wailed, nearly brought to tears.

His eyes burned with sleeplessness, and his whiskers grew un-evenly over his pale cheeks.

Gordon and Zera looked at his wares and bought a used Nietzsche and a paperback of Plato's *Republic*, leaving a nearly un-opened volume of Wittgenstein's *Tractatus* despite the seller's offer to discount it another fifty percent.

"That was what ruined me," the man said. "After Wittgenstein, what is there anyone could do?"

"Get an honest job, I suppose," Gordon blurted, surprising himself by this disdainful attitude toward academia.

"You sound as if the bloom has gone off the rose of university life," Zera said.

"I think it has, and now I realize it was even before all this amphora business started. Because I was a good student, I somehow thought that was my niche, especially because so many other people thought so as well."

"You're young; you have time to choose a different path."

"I could get really good at making license plates," he said.

Back at his flat, they laid out the things Gordon would take with him on his clandestine visit to the classics department.

"Do you want me to come with you?" Zera asked.

"I can't expect you to get in trouble, too. Plus I might need to call you if I'm arrested."

"Arrested again," she corrected.

He shrugged like Arnold Schwarzenegger or Bruce Willis and started packing the gym bag.

"I know; a man's gotta do what a man's gotta do," she said.

He finished packing and Zera left, but not before giving him her digital camera. He set his alarm for two A.M. but barely slept. His plan was to go in, snoop around until six o'clock, hide in the men's room and change clothes, then leave when the building was opened for the day.

It was just before three A.M. when he got to campus. He made sure to go between buildings rather than the main walkways. A patrol car was heading away from him on College Walk, and after it was well in the distance, he hurried to the entrance of the classics building. The keys were well marked and he had been with other professors when they unlocked the building after hours. He got through the front door easily and re-locked it. On the wall at one side was the control panel and a light flashed telling him he had one minute to disable the alarm. He prayed they hadn't changed the key or the procedure when he inserted the small notched key. It turned and the flashing light went off. If someone looked through the glass door they would see it was disarmed, but he chanced that no one would be paying that much attention if nothing else were amiss. There were security cameras, but he had masked his face and head with a black scarf, ninja style, and walked through the inner double doors.

He checked the Penniman wing which now had a new, separate alarm, a classic case of locking the barn doors after the horse got out, he mused. But he knew there was little that could help him there and moved on to the faculty offices which could be opened with a master key that was in the secretary's desk.

Dr. Longstreet's office was much as it had been, papers laid out, correspondence to be answered, and a picture of Longstreet with his wife and children when they were all younger posed against the backdrop of temple ruins in Sicily.

Gordon went through the other offices, saving Fontana's for last. Once inside, he shined his flashlight about, disappointed that it was the usual assortment of books, files, and notes. The middle drawer was locked, however, and there was no key hidden in the usual places; the ceremonial Columbia coffee mug on the shelf, under the blotter, in another drawer which had a tin box filled with paper clips, loose change, and political campaign buttons. Gordon got under the desk and saw that, as it was ancient and rickety, the middle drawer was not that tightly secured. There were screws which could be removed to disassemble the tracks which held the drawer in place. He got out his screwdriver and carefully removed the tracks, then lowered the drawer.

There were envelopes, pencils, some computer disks, and a glass paperweight with "Orlando, Florida", complete with frolicking dolphins disporting themselves. He booted up the laptop to look at the computer disks, but all that was there was a draft of a manuscript for a book on Greek culture in the age of Pericles, and not very original at that, Gordon thought.

He was about to replace all the items and secure the drawer back in place when he noticed an address book. There were names in different color inks, and little stars or circles next to some of them. It was not a directory of academic names, he realized. "Ginger Carey" was one name, and "Claudia" without a surname leading off the C entries. Phone numbers were scratched out sometimes and replaced with other numbers. "Rosalind" was all one number had next to it, but there were four stars next to her name, doodled in with a red felt-tipped marker.

Under M he saw "Madame Lucinda's" and a Manhattan phone number. He searched the name on his smartphone, and a name with the same number came up. It advertised itself as an escort service for "upscale professional men", and boasted that it was discrete, confidential, and satisfaction was guaranteed.

Gordon surmised that he was looking at Fontana's "little black book". Disgusting enough, but not proof he was a thief. "Except", Gordon heard ringing in his ears. The exception was motive. As Frank Kelley had pointed out, that was the key. If Fontana was into call girls, prostitutes, and pleasures of the flesh generally, that would be reason enough to need to find more cash to finance his hobby. Gordon was innocent of the particulars of the flesh trade, but suspected that high-end ladies of the evening were beyond a professor's salary. But how to prove that this was the link was the problem.

Gordon took the book to the hallway and photocopied all of the pages. He rushed back to the office and replaced the book, reassembled the drawer, locked everything, and went to the men's room to change into street clothes. It almost six-thirty in the morning now and he remembered the alarm, but thought to leave it off and let whoever was opening think the previous night's closer had forgotten to set it.

At seven he heard people in the corridors and after waiting another hour, standing on a toilet in the men's room so that his feet would not be visible, he walked out with his gym bag. Some students were milling around for an early class, and he casually walked out the door without creating suspicion or anyone's notice.

He walked back home and called Zera with his report.

"No one saw you?"

"I was tantamount to invisible," he said.

"It worries me that you are too intuitively good at this. I think you even liked it."

Gordon didn't answer, but he knew the rush of adrenalin he felt exceeded any joy he ever knew from doing translations of Latin odes or Greek dramas. He slept like a dead man that afternoon, but in the evening he got up ready for his next move. He would stake out Fontana's apartment and follow him. Gordon found out he lived on Claremont Avenue in university housing, and he waited across the street for two evenings wearing sunglasses, a baseball cap, and even a cashier's jacket he had lifted from D'Avolio's grocery store. His quarry did not appear, but on the third night, at about eight o'clock, Fontana emerged from his building. He hailed a cab on Broadway, but got away before Gordon could catch another.

It occurred to him that if he was going to track Fontana to some fleshpot, he would need to start on the far end first. He reviewed his copy of the address book and saw "The Touch of Silk" noted as being just north of Times Square, and learned it was a strip club from a web search. The next night he staked himself outside the club and a little after eight, a cab pulled out and Fontana got out and went inside.

Gordon had never been in such a place, but waited a few minutes and then went to the entrance. "Ten dollar cover," a large man standing at the door said. Gordon forked over a ten-dollar bill and went inside. He went to the back of the club and took a seat. He could see Fontana sitting down in the first row by the stage. There were tuxedoed bouncers, loud music, and cocktail waitresses in slinky dresses working the crowd of men gathered there. A young woman in a blue dress came by and put her hand on Gordon's shoulder.

"What are you having, handsome?" she said with a smile.

Gordon was flustered but said, "Beer, please," as the first thing that came to mind.

The disco music and strobe lights amused Gordon. The customers were focused on the stage where a well-endowed redhead in a G-string was climbing a pole, twisting herself around it, and finally hanging head down.

The waitress brought his beer in a bottle; it was twelve dollars and he gave her a ten and a five telling her to keep the change.

"Thanks; if you want a private dance, let me know and I'll send someone over."

Gordon calculated how much an evening at a place like this would cost. Just then a new song came on and the announcer's voice said, "And now, a wonderful lady from South America. You will love her exotic moves; please welcome Tanya the Piranha!"

Hoots and cheers broke out as the young woman took the stage. The crowd were mostly men in suits. Fontana wore a silk shirt and jacket and sipped a cocktail as he watched the show.

The dancer swayed and slithered, finally sitting on the stage where the men at the front could see everything. She slapped her thighs and buttocks firmly, stuck out her tongue, and finally tossed off her G-string, shaking her breasts and pushing her pelvis forward.

This was vile, Gordon thought. It demeaned women, it was a crime against the dignity of sex, it was just appalling, he told himself, but when a chair nearer the stage became empty, he took his drink and moved closer.

When she was finished, the announcer said, "And for those of you who would like a private dance, please see Oscar Hammerstein the 3rd, director of the VIP room."

Gordon looked to where everyone else was looking and saw a man in a tuxedo who was standing to acknowledge the introduction. He was about six foot three and built like a boxer. His head was shaved and he sported a mustache and goatee, and a gaze severe enough to deter anyone from violating any point of the club's etiquette.

Gordon watched two more dancers, Santana and Brandy, and resisted buying a drink for each of the several girls who came up and asked him if he wanted company. Fontana was intent on the show and did not look in Gordon's direction, but he seemed a man not particularly interested in any of the girls more than another.

A redhead was followed by a brunette and Gordon found all of them amazingly athletic in their performances. Girls like Jane or even Zera were not of the same cut as these women who seemed to have no scruple or inhibition.

A dancer in a flimsy outfit walked over to Gordon and sat down.

'I'm Sapphire; what's your name?"

"Jimmy," Gordon said.

"Well, Jimmy, would you like a lap dance?"

"Mm, I suppose, "Gordon said hesitantly.

"Let's go over to the leather couches, then."

"How much does it cost?" Gordon asked, feeling for once he grasped the essence of New York.

"Forty dollars for one song," she said, and she took Gordon by the hand. He gave her the money and she sat him down and began her dance, sitting on his lap, then getting up and kneeling in front of him, moving her hips and shoulders, letting her long hair fall on his face when was she was perched above him. She was very pretty and well built, he thought, although her conversational skills were lacking.

When the song was over he thanked her, and as she hung about without leaving he realized he should give her a tip in addition to what he had already paid. He peeled off a ten and handed it to her.

She leaned forward and whispered to him, "There is a VIP room upstairs; we could go there if you want. It's more private. I can touch you and you can touch me," she said.

"How much is that?"

"Seven hundred for an hour," she said. "Plus a tip."

"How much would that be?"

She smiled. "I would hate to limit your generosity."

"Maybe another time," Gordon replied, going back to where he had been sitting. This paid-for-exchange had been the closest thing to physical contact with a woman he had since coming to New York.

He watched Fontana watching the show, but as the stripper picked up the dollar bills tossed onto the stage, the announcer let it be known that what they had been waiting for all evening was about to happen. With a list of superlatives to preface matters, a stupendously statuesque blonde appeared just as the announcer said, "Direct from Las Vegas, we give you Tiffany Z."

Whistles and thunderous applause greeted her, and Gordon could see Fontana spring to attention. She was fair-skinned with long blonde hair and green eyes, and a profile that the light accentuated. Her hips, breasts, and legs all conspired to a notion of absolute beauty, and all eyes were soon on her.

She danced and gyrated, and when she removed her sequined brassiere, Gordon thought he would faint at the sheer perfection of what he saw.

"A male fantasy," he heard a voice in his head say, no doubt from some panel discussion on gender he had been forced to endure, a female professor denouncing pornography. "How wonderful," a counter-voice said, and both voices vied for dominance in his head, forming a chorus that both chided him and cheered him on. He felt anti-intellectual, unenlightened, primitive, and politically incorrect. He assured himself that he did respect women, but as he said that, he was deliriously drunk on the smoothness of Tiffany's skin and the firmness of her buttocks as she lasciviously bounced them in his view.

Her dance was all things to all men, judging by the ample tips they stuffed in her garter, but none more than Michael Fontana, who in an apparent state of transfixed bliss, folded a hundred-dollar bill and slowly slid it under the red silk band on her left thigh.

When Tiffany was finished, she put on her G-string and half robe and went off stage, soon to re-emerge and head in Fontana's direction. They chatted a few minutes and Fontana held her hand, oozing his reptilian charm against the backdrop of thumping rock music. Finally, she led him to the VIP room where Oscar Hammerstein the 3rd and a prissy young man with a bucket of champagne tended to him in return for more money changing hands. Gordon waited another half hour, then another again before Fontana came back out into the main room. Gordon slipped out, wending his way through the crowd, until he was on the street and safely away from the club. He estimated that the professor had spent over a thousand dollars that evening, and could not wait to share this intelligence with Zera. He called her on his cell phone from a pizza parlor whose weary employees were occupied by the television mounted on the wall, leaving the customers to themselves.

"I'm not far away; I have to come by and tell you what I've just seen."

He hung up before she could answer and felt a certain Dashiell Hammett in his tone. For once he was more Robert Mitchum than Pee-Wee Herman. Gordon hurried to Zera's flat five blocks up and two avenues across. When he arrived at Zera's, he told of following Fontana and what he had discovered.

"The man's a pervert," Gordon said vengefully, as if that explained everything.

"I'd say you're a pervert, too, then," she answered sourly, plainly unwilling to accept any theory that incriminated Fontana.

Gordon was crestfallen and silent while Zera picked up odd sheets of paper, newspaper columns, magazines, and other debris that cluttered her flat.

The quiet was finally broken when she asked, "Have you eaten yet?"

"No," he said, "but it seems we're always eating."

Zera shrugged. "I do it three times a day."

They left the flat and walked five blocks to a Polish restaurant that advertised sausage, potatoes, and cabbage.

"You would eat anything," Gordon said as two steaming plates were brought to them.

"Aren't fat, starch, salt, and lard the four major food groups?"

After they ate Zera was at least more amenable to listening to Gordon's conjectures.

"If he has a taste for expensive women, it would certainly be a reason to steal."

"But he could jeopardize his academic career; that would be pretty stupid, wouldn't it? To throw it all away for a stripper?" Zera countered

Gordon let out a laugh. "Hello? 'The Blue Angel' with Marlena Dietrich? The elderly and lonely professor falls in love with a cabaret singer and makes himself an object of ridicule. It's actually a very old tale."

Zera remembered the film and was forced to agree. "Man loses his head over a piece of tail," she said.

"You can always find the vulgar way to say things," he replied.

"What happened to that private school propriety your parents paid for?"

She bristled. "I've been trying to overcome propriety ever since. I aim for authenticity, the vocabulary of the common man."

They left the restaurant and she said, "Fontana did have some reputation as a ladies' man when I was at Columbia. Not with students, but just generally. I wouldn't think he would have to pay for what he wanted."

"From what I'm learning about life, people pay for a lot of things they otherwise wouldn't have."

"Probably another pleasant aspect of being married," Zera said. "That sex at home fades very quickly and this sends people looking elsewhere."

"You're awfully gloomy about marriage," Gordon said. "Have you ever been in that institution?"

"No."

"Would you ever want to be?"

She smiled and answered, 'I'll take that as a general question, not a proposal. My answer would be that it depends."

"On...?"

"Attaining philosophical union and trans-theoretical understanding."

Gordon said, "Sounds like a riddle to me."

Zera reached for a cigarette, put it back and said, "So what are you going to do with this information you've gleaned on Fontana?"

"Find out more; if he's just a sex maniac, it is of no use to me. But if he is using money from the amphora theft, that will be my exoneration."

Zera crossed her arms and stood with her feet planted apart, like a fighter ready to step into action. "It's not that my mind is closed to this possibility, but it seems too easy to suspect someone you disliked in the first place."

"Maybe, maybe not. In these past few weeks I have come to think my instincts are sounder than I have given myself credit for as a rule."

Gordon left her and walked to Broadway to catch a cab. The smell of rotting refuse in the summer heat and a dog barking stood in contrast to the pleasant summer air and full moon. When he first arrived in New York he would take the train downtown and walk in the evenings near the Empire State Building and look up if the moon was visible, thinking of all that the city had been in American history and culture, romanticizing that his time there would make him sophisticated and rise above his prairie simplicity. Now he felt as if all that aspiration was being trampled into defeat from which there was no recovery.

A torn and tattered Somali cabbie picked Gordon up and flew north like the winged horse Pegasus. The driver chatted with his friends on his cell phone as he turned corners recklessly and made end runs to pass cars moving too slowly for his tastes.

Once home, Gordon sat in his armchair thinking about his next move. What he needed was corroboration, something else to buttress his judgment that the professor could be the thief. Merely thinking Fontana a sleaze gave Gordon satisfaction, but he needed a better get-out-of-jail card than mere moral degeneracy.

"Amo, amas, amat…"

G ORDON STOPPED FOLLOWING FONTANA AND merely waited for him to show up each evening at the strip club, which he inevitably did three nights in a row between eight and nine o'clock. He would spend a few hours, including several private sessions with Tiffany, then leave to go home. On the fourth night, Thursday, when Fontana had not arrived by ten, Gordon went inside and asked a dancer named Angelique about Tiffany and was told she had the night off.

He described Fontana and said he was someone who came often to see Tiffany.

"Him; he's got it bad for her," Angelique said.

"It isn't the scene that has him hooked," Gordon told Zera later, "but this girl in particular."

Zera conceded that Fontana's visitations to the club would cause anyone to run through a great deal of money, but that he might have a trust fund.

"Does everyone who lives well in this city have inherited money?"

"Most that I know," Zera said.

The next day Gordon sat down with pen and paper and estimated the monthly expenses of a man who dropped thousands of dollars a week for a woman in addition to all the normal expenses of living in New York. He concluded that Frank Kelley's dictum had been satisfied; here was a man who needed more money than he earned and had the opportunity to make some through theft.

Since this was something he couldn't establish in a definitive way, he thought he would rely upon the most time-tested of sources for corroboration of his view of Fontana's character: gossip, rumor, and the opinion of one's neighbors. He remembered that Professor Longstreet also lived on Claremont Avenue, and decided he owed a long-postponed visit to the professor's wife. He looked them up online and found their names listed: James P. and Lenore M.

He punched in the number, amazed at yet another way he had become a New Yorker; the willingness to calculate how much use a person could be to him. The phone rang, then again, then a third time, and just when he was expecting the answering machine to break in, a woman's voice spoke.

"Hello?"

"Hello," he said, clearing his throat. "Is this Mrs. Longstreet?"

"Ye-es," she said in a drawn-out assent, ready to slam the phone down if he turned out to be a salesman or other form of telepest.

"This is Gordon Bauer, one of your husband's graduate students. We spoke at the service and you said you would like it if I called."

A long, chilly silence made Gordon regret what he had done. He bit his lip as he waited for her reply. She must know, he thought, in a way native New Yorkers do, when the caller is selling you something.

"Gordon," she finally said in a beam of recognition. "How sweet of you to call." Her tone was raspy and deep, a Chivas Regal and Virginia Slims voice that would chase a cockroach from a cheese platter.

They talked for a while and he asked if he could come to visit her. She was charmed and offered to be at home that very afternoon. Gordon hung up and then took a long shower, trying to strategize how he would get her to tell him all she knew of Fontana. After lunch, he made a hurried trip to the Amsterdam Avenue Florist Shop to buy a small bouquet of flowers. An ancient man in a green apron attempted to find out what sort of arrangement he wanted.

"Nothing funereal," he said.

"For a funeral?" the old man barked.

"No," Gordon said. "It's for a friend."

"You frendt ist a boy or a girl?"

"A girl, a woman really."

The flower seller smiled and winked. "I make you up somethink nice."

Gordon left with a bouquet in hand and walked deliberately to Claremont Avenue considering his approach.

It was a warm, sunny day and even the beggars were cheerful. A hot dog vendor pushed his wagon to a shadier spot on the corner, and an exuberant man with cheap leather wallets and belts spread on a blanket touted his wares to passersby.

"Very good wallets here," he said, looking at Gordon.

Gordon thought as he walked past that it appeared to be the same man who was selling umbrellas a few days before, and watches the week previous.

When Gordon arrived at Mrs. Longstreet's address, he rang the bell and was admitted. Once upstairs and inside her apartment, he found the widow neither merry nor melancholic, just tipsy.

"Would you like a drink?" she asked, and walked to the kitchen to put ice in a glass.

"Just water, please, Mrs. Longstreet."

She gasped and put a hand over her heart in a mocking way. "Please; it's Lenore," she croaked. "I'm not old enough to be your mother."

She poured some water from a pitcher for Gordon as he calculated her age. He knew she was younger than her late husband and had grown children, but she was well-preserved with a good figure. He guessed to himself that she was about fifty-three or four, which of course made her exactly old enough to be his mother. She floated back into the room with her drink, gin and tonic. Her ash blonde hair was well-coifed, and she wore a fitted blouse that accentuated her breasts, and her skirt stopped at her knees revealing toned legs.

"How thoughtful of you to come," she said, taking a seat on the couch next to him at a distance Gordon felt was twelve inches closer than polite and just six short of outright seduction. He didn't know what to make of her, watching as she lit a cigarette, took a sip of her drink, and launched into a monologue about her late husband. He was a prince, she said, but was unappreciated by the university. Dr. Longstreet was still mentally active and capable at sixty-five and should never have been pushed out of his chairmanship.

"He ran that department splendidly," she said, "unlike that donkey in man's britches who chairs it now."

Gordon realized he had hit pay dirt; she disliked Fontana so much that she could not even say his name. Pumping her for details would not take much, he thought, but as she inched a bit closer to him, he wondered if his falling on the word "pumping" reflected his worst fears of what he would have to do to keep her talking.

Lenore went on about Fontana's treachery and double-dealing, his ambition, and his reputation with women.

"What is his wife like?" Gordon asked

"Who knows?" Lenore Longstreet said dismissively. "They say she was a barmaid in Cambridge, England when he met her while on sabbatical. She has no brains and no interests, just huge tits. And she's either wife number two or number three depending on whom you believe."

Gordon listened as she continued to run Fontana down. She was witty and mordant in her observations, but she revealed more about herself than the object of her scorn. She had two more drinks on top of what she had already consumed. She was a lonely woman, he felt, whose widowhood could easily slide into complete bitterness. Her eyes were bright blue, and she had fair skin and a pleasant smile when briefly she flashed it. Gordon wondered about the frustrations of being an academic wife, of being the moon to someone else's sun if you had no independent career.

"More water?" Mrs. Longstreet asked, taking Gordon's glass.

"Yes, please."

When she returned she crossed her legs and slouched closer to him. He felt an impulse of desire, wondering how his long year of celibacy was now making a woman her age seem attractive.

He had to remember his mission and said, "I heard Fontana's wife was an heiress," Gordon said, lying in a burst of creativity he never knew he possessed.

"Ha!" she exclaimed. "Do they say that now? I've never heard it. He must have started that rumor to make her seem more than she is. Odd, when you come to think of it. If he married her because she was a tart, he would feel some embarrassment in academic circles, but if he had married her for her money, that would be respectable. I don't think he has a penny because she doesn't work and they have a son, plus him paying for the other two brats from the first wife who don't live with him."

"He has three children?"

"Vile little monsters," she said taking another sip.

Gordon was pleased to hear this, for a man with expenses plus bad habits would need a constant supply of cash.

"But let's not talk about him. It upsets me too much. He's the one who greased the skids on Bill, the conniving bastard."

"I've never liked him myself," Gordon said quietly.

"Are you going to become a professor, too?"

"I'm not sure, "Gordon said sorrowfully. "There seem to be things that would prevent it, and lately I'm not sure it's how I want to spend my life."

"Oh, don't," she said, becoming agitated. "It's a terrible thing to waste one's mind, and you do. Teaching becomes routine, and people spend their days in meetings and writing ghastly papers no one reads. It's just tenure scribbling. I wish Bill had become an archaeologist. He loved the digs on Crete and Sicily the few times he was able to go. But you need independent means or continual grants to make it a career. It's cruel."

With that she started sobbing, repeating "cruel" several times, and when her tears kept falling, Gordon reached his arm around her shoulder and her head fell on his chest.

"There now," he said, thinking how Laurence Olivier would

comfort a woman. He had no firsthand experience with the subject since he had never broken anyone's heart.

"Oh, I feel so *low*," she said, clutching onto Gordon, the last word being spoken almost in a baritone. She lifted her head and their faces were inches apart. He smelled her perfume and hair spray mingling with the whiff of liquor. Having sex with this woman would no doubt be something that would disgust him in the morning, as well as violate every principle he thought he held. But as her hand stroked his chest, a year of monastic abstinence turned every perspective on its head. She was a woman and she was alive, breathing, and desirous of him. Since she seemed to be experiencing no moral qualms over what was to happen next, he thought it silly to be thinking rather than acting.

Their mouths came together in unison, and the rest happened by instinct undefeated by long disuse. Her tongue probed for his and he grew more passionate. His willpower by then had dissolved like a sugar cube in hot tea. Hands reached for buckles, buttons, and zippers, and soon they were lying naked on the couch. He saw blue veins against white skin and the stretch marks on her abdomen, things previously unknown to him. They writhed and bounced, and she groaned as he picked up the pace and took his earlobe between her teeth and nipped and licked gently at it. He found it stimulating for its novelty, but terrifying if it was the prelude to something involving actual pain. She arched her hips after that, then clawed his back and let out a moan simultaneous with his moment of pleasure, and when they finally rested from their labors, she held him close to her, the lacquered stiffness of her hair resting against his cheek.

She got up a while later to make herself another drink, which was mostly gin and precious little tonic. She took him to the bedroom where they lay under a sheet, the window air conditioner clanking softly as it blew cool air in their direction. She talked about her late husband and the two children she despaired would ever become adults, although they were in their twenties. She blamed herself for this, as her husband spent the thirty years of their marriage blissfully unaware of very little not found in the ancient world.

"Poor Billy," she said. "I miss him so much even though he drove me crazy."

Gordon tried to console her, but she broke into a coughing fit as she tried to light a cigarette. She had a few puffs, crushed it out, and went for more liquor. Once back in bed, she reached under the covers for his now soldier-standing-at-ease, which responded to the invitation by coming to attention.

"Should I do what the young girls do today?" she asked impishly.

Gordon was baffled as he had little clue about what the young girls did until her head disappeared under the sheet. He sighed and surrendered to pleasures unknown with Jane, whose Wisconsin Catholic background had made her decidedly non-experimental when it came to such matters.

After that, Lenore got up for yet more alcohol and a trip to the bathroom. She came back to bed, drank down what she had poured, and proceeded to fall into a dead, drunken sleep. She lay on her back and soon her steady breathing broke into a grunting snore. Her hair was tousled and her lipstick smeared and she smelled of perspiration and gin. Gordon thought the most tactful thing to do then would be to leave. It was almost seven o'clock and the summer evening sun was casting its shadows on the walls and bookshelves in the front room where he went to retrieve his clothes and shoes. He had done as much comforting as he felt obliged to do for one day, and had gotten some useful information. He got dressed and took his glass to the dishwasher but left hers on the night table next to her bed as he looked in on her before leaving.

"Perhaps she'll think she dreamt the whole thing," he thought.

She snored in fits, her mouth gaping open, then snapped her lips together and went back into deeper sleep. Gordon felt sorry for her, and then for himself, and finally for the whole human predicament. Sex when you are young was a romantic allure to trick the species into reproducing, but in a few short decades is this what it could turn into: an exchange for pity or comfort leaving both parties feeling shortchanged? It was a colossal joke of nature as far as he could see, although he held some faint hope that it could be more.

He went home and called Zera, anxious to figure out what he should do next to connect the dots between Fontana's character and financial problems with the actual theft.

"Why don't you meet me for dinner tomorrow night?" she said. She suggested a place called "Ulan Bator", which he knew was the capital of Mongolia. She said it would be an experiment he should be open to. He fretted about what Mongolian cuisine might be all the next day: frozen yak, horse meat?

He met Zera at the appointed time the next night on Eighth Avenue. She wore a blue skirt with a green blouse and a saffron-hued scarf. Her earrings were yellow, green, and brown speckled drops of polished stone which looked like some Amazonian insect or perhaps fishing lures. He felt oddly less susceptible to her, having had sex the day before. The wild horses were resting, at least temporarily.

He looked at the menu posted in the window and saw a waiter bringing a steaming plate of colorless mutton dumplings. Looking at the menu he said, "I think duck brains are the next course; no way are we eating here."

He took her by the arm and headed for the crosswalk. "There is a nice Chinese place across the street; we're going there. China is as close to Mongolia as I want to be."

They went across the street and sat in a booth where he took out a piece of paper and unfolded it. Persons, places, clues, and events were charted, and Gordon began connecting the dots.

"Listen to me," he began, moving his pen as he took her through his scenario. "Fontana is romancing a woman he can't afford; that's the motive. The amphora disappeared, and who knows what else they haven't discovered, that is the crime. His opportunity was next to useless security and nearly unrestricted access to the amphora, even when it was locked in the vault. The Stanopoulos Galleries are his fence and were used to help set me up; I think that part with the money planted in my desk was a convenient afterthought strategy once I fell under suspicion. And lastly, since the police and the medical examiner have concluded Longstreet died of a heart attack, I am thinking perhaps Fontana and he got into some argument, Longstreet keeled over, and instead of calling 911, he saw his moment and took the amphora then and there."

Gordon connected the last dot and Zera sat there, her chin resting on one hand.

"So what piece is left?" he said, addressing the silence.

"Proving he did it," Zera said, looking a cross between bored and annoyed.

Gordon looked back at her with the same expression. "I have."

He then told Zera of his follow-up trips to the strip club and what he had observed of Fontana and all the money he was spending.

"I still think it's conjecture," she said.

"What do I have to do; get him to admit it?

"That would help, but I am puzzled why he would throw everything away for a stripper."

"Human passions are irrational," Gordon said, thinking both of Greek tragedies and his afternoon with Lenore Longstreet.

"I'm not sure."

"Let's go back to 'The Blue Angel'; can you download it from a service?"

"Yes, I suppose," she said, and after they ate they went to her place and proceeded to watch the film fed to her television from her laptop. It was a 1930 production in German with English subtitles. Zera and Gordon watched as Lola-Lola, the vamp singer, seduced the old professor, who gave up his position and all respectability to pursue her.

"It was decades ago, but human nature doesn't change."

"That's what all you classicists believe," she said. "I'll have to digest this," she said. "And speaking of digesting, let's go have cake or something. I'm still hungry."

They found a Viennese café and sat across from one another. Zera was in a reflective mood and talked about her parents, her therapist's views of her situation, and her goals and ideals. Gordon found a certain tenderness in her at times, which somehow existed in tandem with the hardness of her manner. Gordon was as caught as ever in the undertow of her offbeat magnetism, and as they got up to leave, he kissed her.

She didn't turn her head away and when their lips moved apart she began, "Gordon..."

"No comments," he said. "I didn't ask you for anything."

She smiled and he walked her home. That night he slept fitfully, thinking how he could unmask Fontana, and also how it could be that he was in love with Zera when she would never love him in return.

The next day he got up early and turned on his little television. A news reporter with her long blonde hair pulled back and in army field jacket rather than a dress was delivering what was apparently a hastily filed report from Ululibad.

"The revolutionaries, long holed up in the mountains, have made a dramatic breakout from their position. The daring pre-dawn attacks on several army garrisons have resulted in the whole northern section falling to the rebels. The insurgents are reported to be only thirty kilometers from the capital."

A few minutes later a knock on Gordon's door revealed the three Ululistanis standing there, elated and weeping.

"You have heard the good news, yes?" Hamid said with excitement.

"Yes," Gordon said, but was quickly interrupted as they spoke hurriedly in English and Ululistani.

"Hamid and Khalil are leaving right now to go back home and join the fighting. I've been ordered to stay here and coordinate press releases and lobby the U.N. for recognition," Ali said. Gordon noticed a sheaf of papers in his hand.

"We have an open phone line and fax to headquarters," he announced proudly, as if these two modern devices conferred legitimacy on anyone who used them.

"We do need a favor, though," Hamid interrupted.

"I wouldn't be very good at being a revolutionary," Gordon demurred.

"No, we need you to drive our taxi back from Newark Airport and bring it to the depot."

Gordon looked at them blankly and realized he would be driving a cab from New Jersey to New York without a permit, something probably a crime.

"We are late and have to leave right away," Khalil said. "Ali has to go downtown and we have no other way to get the cab back."

Their beseeching eyes convinced Gordon that any illegalities could be excused by the law of necessity, or at the very least he could be in no greater trouble than he was in already. They drove to Newark in a fever pitch of excitement, telling Gordon how he was helping in the birth of a nation.

"Maybe there will be a statue of me in a taxi cab, sort of latter day Paul Revere without the horse," he mused.

The traffic was merciless going out, but after he dropped them at the curb (to kisses on both his cheeks by the men), he found the return trip even worse. Making sure his light was off to avoid being flagged down, he crept back to Manhattan in a stream of cars. When he was only a few blocks from the garage on the West Side near the piers, a whim overcame him which was totally out of character. It would perhaps be his only chance in a lifetime to do this, so why not? He slammed the gas pedal to the floor on a green light, accelerating to fifty miles an hour, passed three cars and a taxi, made a sharp left in front of a truck, swerved to avoid a pushcart crossing the street, then slammed the brakes on at a red light, stopping three inches from the car in front of him at the intersection and just as close to a BMW sedan beside him.

"You crazy idiot," the driver of the BMW screamed at him.

"Asshole," Gordon shouted back, waving his middle finger.

When the light changed, he drove the cab into the taxi lot, adrenalin still pumping from his gesture of contempt for civilization and good order. He ran inside the garage, dropped the keys with a hasty explanation while not mentioning who he was, and ran for the door as quickly as his feet would carry him. He stopped running a few blocks later and saw a jet high above him in the sky, perhaps even the Ululistanis' flight. He wondered how the revolution would fare, and how they would adapt to not being in New York.

Once he got home, his mind turned to his own dilemma. He needed something tangible to take to the police and pondered what he could do. It was the last day of July now and the weather was sweltering. Summer school would be ending and the campus would soon empty out until Labor Day. Despite being barred from Mandeville Hall, he entered the building late one afternoon when the secretaries would have left, but before students for evening classes would arrive. He had the keys and was thinking of entering Fontana's office again. Fontana had a class that ran from 4:30 to 6:30 four days a week, and he would be upstairs in one of the lecture rooms. Gordon walked down the corridor to the faculty offices, fingering the keys while looking behind him. He turned the corner and was startled as he saw Fontana on the other side of a glass door entering the corridor from the opposite. He pulled back around the corner and thought to get out of sight as quickly as he could. The men's room was there and he ducked in, going to the last stall where he stood on the seat to avoid being visible. He would wait there for ten minutes, then leave.

The plan seemed perfect except that someone else entered a few moments later. He heard a voice and realized it was Fontana, talking on his cell phone.

"Tiffany, please," he said. "You've kept me waiting for all I desire. I cannot stand it any longer."

There was silence, then a few words from Fontana, then more silence.

It was clear to Gordon that Fontana wanted to have sex with her and was quite willing to pay. He would die otherwise, he said.

"Twenty-five thousand dollars?" he said in a shocked tone. "Why I could buy three of the best whores in New York for that!"

Another silence was followed by blubbering Fontana apologies. "No, of course, I didn't mean you were a whore, just that it is a lot of money."

This went on for another minute and finally Fontana sounded joyful. "For a whole week of you? That would be worth it."

They concluded the deal by Fontana saying that he wanted the first time to be in his office. He gave instructions on how she was to dress; like a college freshman just in from some small town. Her hair in a braid, jeans, and a tight jersey.

"See you at seven o'clock tomorrow night here; Mandeville Hall, room 207. I can't wait; your honey hair, your perfect breasts…"

The conversation ended and Gordon heard Fontana leave the men's room. He waited and racked his brain figuring how he would catch Fontana in the act of forking over the money he no doubt received for the amphora. Now standing outside of the stall, he looked up at the ceiling and saw it was just Styrofoam panels. A mop with a long handle stood in the corner, and he took it and pushed up to raise one of the panels. As he suspected, the panels were merely a drop ceiling in the old building. Above it there were another five feet to the actual ceiling, with wooden beams running across and parallel. It dawned on him then that he could slip into Fontana's office before him, get up into the beams and watch and listen through a peephole, and even record the transaction between Fontana and his Lola-Lola on his smart phone.

He went home and called Zera, telling her his plan and at last she believed him about Fontana.

"But you'll need a corroborating wit-ness," she said in a sing-song voice. "And if I'm with you, I'll also get the scoop of my career."

They laid out their plans for the following evening: to get into the building, hide out until Fontana and Tiffany were transacting their business, and get it all recorded before taking it to Detective Sabatini.

Gordon was exhilarated by his burglar's courage. The Fates, the mythic women who measured, cut, and wove the threads of one's life, had brought him to this dangerous precipice. It would be all or nothing now. He would either catch the thief, or end his academic career in a blaze of infamy. He would snip this strand of bad luck these ladies had woven for him. He needed to become a man of action, a Greek hero who could sometimes propitiate the gods, but when necessary thumb his nose at them as well.

XI

"Deus...ex machina."

Z ERA ARRIVED AT GORDON'S FLAT at four o'clock the next day
with a large cup of iced coffee.

"Maybe that's not such a good idea," Gordon said, pointing to
the coffee where Zera had put it down on the old second hand table.

"You're worried about marking up the table?" she laughed.

"No, you drinking all of that."

"I need to stay awake," she protested.

Gordon sighed. "But you'll also need to relieve yourself of it, and
we'll be up in the rafters for hours."

"Shit," she exclaimed, suddenly aware of the problem.

"No, piss," he said with a laugh. It was the first time he had let
his reserve fall with her. He realized that was his main problem, always worrying what others might think. Now he was in a distinctly,
"Fuck 'em if they can't take a joke" frame of mind that day and he
liked it.

He went back to packing his bag, and Zera dumped all but
a few mouthfuls of the coffee in the sink. They ran through their

checklist, packed the gym bag, then left for the campus. August had begun with heavy air and the sun shone through a dense, damp haze. Summer school was in its final week, and students crossed the neatly manicured walks to Butler Library and the classroom buildings. At five-thirty Gordon and Zera entered Mandeville Hall, looking like graduate students with their backpacks.

"Let's each have a last pass at the loo," he said as they were by the restrooms. They emerged a few minutes later, checked the hallways for security people, but the building was quite empty except for two lecture rooms on the second floor where classes were going on, including the one taught by Fontana.

They slipped into the janitorial closet and got a stepladder, then Gordon carried it to Fontana's doorway, unlocked the door, and took the ladder inside with Zera right behind him. They closed the door and locked it.

He opened the ladder up and set it under the place where a thumbtack was stuck to one of the drop panels. Climbing to the fifth step of the ladder, he reached up and pushed the panel open.

"They mark them for that reason," he said. "It's for maintenance access where there will be a beam above."

He climbed up into the opening, holding onto one of the beams to support himself.

Zera handed two backpacks with their supplies and photo-graphic and recording equipment up to Gordon, then turned out the lights and shone her flashlight to climb up to the opening where Gordon helped her to enter. Gordon had tied a rope around the top step of the ladder and when they were both up in the rafters, he pulled the ladder up, folded it as it came up with Zera's help, and placed it on two cross beams. He then replaced the ceiling panel and turned on his flashlight to look at his watch.

They cut two holes in the ceiling tile for each of them to have a view of the middle of the room, as well as the professor's desk and chair. Zera would run the video camera from one spot, and Gordon would record on his smartphone a few feet away, able then to cover most of the office between them.

"We still have at least an hour, but I wanted to be on the safe side."

Being perched as they were was not comfortable, but Gordon noticed a few yards away there was a three-foot wide stone ledge and they gingerly ambled across to where they could sit more easily.

"I need to go back to aerobics," Zera whispered.

"And stop smoking," Gordon added.

"I'll try again if you take me on more dates like this."

He checked his watch now and again. At 6:15 they got back into place above the office, and put their video cam and cell phone on ready to record. Finally, they heard the lock turn and the lights come on. Fontana tidied his desk, paced the floor, and walked back and forth to the window. He went to the desk and found some breath spray, and also a small bottle of cologne which he sprayed liberally on himself, dousing his cheeks, neck, and finally pulling his pants away from his waist, sprayed some downwards to his nether regions. Gordon could practically hear Zera cringe from the tackiness of it.

After twenty more minutes, they heard a knock on the door. It was Tiffany. Zera turned on the video cam pointed down through the hole and Gordon did the same with his phone camera.

"Come into my web, said the spider," Fontana said, opening the door.

She came inside and Fontana kissed her cheek. She wore a cotton pullover jersey, blue jeans, and loafers.

"Is this co-ed enough for you?" she asked.

"A little dated," he replied. "They all wear black now, but you're fine as you are. Kind of the way girls were when I was an undergraduate, which adds to the mood."

"Whatever floats your boat."

"Let me kiss you," Fontana said and reached over for her as she stood at the side of his desk.

Tiffany pulled back. "Why don't we get the financial stuff out of the way first."

He frowned with disappointment. "Is that all you care about?"

"Of course not, but if we get business done first, then we can enjoy ourselves."

Fontana went to his briefcase and laid it on the desk. He opened it and Gordon saw stacks of fifty-dollar bills in neat bundles.

"Didn't I say I'd take good care of you?"

"I'll say," Tiffany said coquettishly.

She counted the money and placed it in an oversized handbag she had.

"I'm sure I can trust you to perform your end of the bargain," Fontana said as he slid out of his shoes, pulled off his shirt, and stepped out of his trousers. He stood there, hairy and saturnine, in a pair of violet bikini briefs.

Gordon was revolted by this, as any man who did not wear white jockeys or at least boxers was depraved.

"So strip, bitch," Fontana said, suddenly turning hostile. "I'm going to work every hole you have until I get my money's worth."

Tiffany stepped back and said, "I had a feeling this was the real you; kinky and violent."

He laughed diabolically, a kind of "Bwa-ha-ha" that had Gordon doing all he could from bursting into laughter.

"You want it this way, so stop playing with me. You're no virgin, you seamy slut."

"I am not a slut," Tiffany said, her voice rising.

"We'll see about that," he said as he lunged for her, but she was too quick and ran to the door, quickly unlocking it as Fontana put one arm around her neck.

The door swung open as he pulled Tiffany backward, and she shouted, "Oscar!"

"Chill professor," said Oscar Hammerstein the 3rd, the bouncer from the club. He stepped inside and closed the door, glowering at Fontana as he held Tiffany.

"Ha," Fontana shouted. "I'm a karate master."

With that Fontana released Tiffany and assumed a martial arts crouch, waving his hands in chop simulation, kicking one foot then the other savagely as he let out breaths of Asian-sounding words. Had he not been standing there in his underwear, Gordon thought it might be half believable.

"Watch him Oscar," Tiffany said.

"Yeah, watch me kick the shit out of you with skill and cunning," Fontana sneered.

"Watch me snuff you with Smith and Wesson," Oscar said, as he drew a nickel-plated revolver from his jacket pocket.

Fontana froze where he stood, his arms in the air pointlessly, and Gordon suspected he knew nothing of karate.

Just then as the three players below were locked in a moment of collective and individual decision-making, there was a cracking sound at Gordon and Zera's feet. The beam they stood on was connected to two cross beams, and ancient brackets on one side had finally given way. The beam let go on one end, not dropping Gordon and Zera directly, but sliding them downward along the beam and through the ceiling almost in slow motion. Ceiling panels crumbled, and Gordon and Zera landed on the floor seven feet below, the debris partially breaking their fall. They lay stunned for a moment and struggled to their feet.

"Who the hell are you?" Oscar said, aiming his gun at them.

"Was this supposed to be 'one does it, two watch for free?'" Tiffany said. "Will the kinkiness never end?"

"I'm a student," Gordon explained. "He stole something valuable to pay you and is trying to frame me for it."

"And who are you?" Tiffany said looking at Zera.

"I'm his girlfriend," Zera said, and Gordon realized she was quick-witted enough not to say she was a reporter.

"Well, I'm sorry you dropped in," Tiffany said, giving Gordon a chill to think they had intended to rob and kill Fontana and now would have to kill him and Zera to cover their tracks.

"Keep them covered," the stripper said as she went to her huge bag and took out handcuffs. She gestured Fontana over to the old iron steam pipe and proceeded to handcuff him to it.

"I didn't bring cuffs for our visitors," she said to Oscar, "but I have rope and duct tape."

She gave them to Oscar. "I'll hold the gun; you tie them back-to-back in these chairs and tape their mouths," she said, and the shaven-headed Oscar grunted obediently. He handed her the gun and pulled two straight wooden chairs together, tying Gordon and Zera to each other and to the chairs back to back, then taped their mouths, but when he turned around he saw Tiffany holding the gun on him.

"Now slip these on your wrist first, then to the steam pipe," she said, pulling another set of handcuffs from the bag in what was apparently a well thought out sting on Oscar that he had never considered.

"Whuh?" the club bouncer said.

"Cuff yourself to the pipe, dimwit. My new life is going to be by myself." She tossed the handcuffs to him and he caught them instinctively.

Oscar started to laugh and walked toward her. "You wouldn't do this to me," he said.

"Try me, asshole," she said. "I'm up to here with you, the club, this city, with being gawked at and pawed like meat. I'm out of here, and unless you want a large caliber vasectomy, you'll do what I tell you."

Oscar stood still in silence, calculating his next move, but when Tiffany cocked the hammer of the gun without a blink and aimed it just below his belt buckle, Oscar backed off, walked slowly to the radiator, and handcuffed himself to it.

"Now I'm not coming over to tape your mouth, Oscar, because you have no incentive to yell. You were here to commit armed robbery, so you won't want the police coming to your assistance."

She turned to Gordon and Zera. "You two were doing something illegal, too, so your best chance is to squirm out of your knots and beat it."

Tiffany gathered up the money, but left the handcuff keys on the desk.

"If you want, you can let poor Oscar go on your way out. What you do with Fontana is your business. I'll be long gone by then." She walked over to Fontana and grabbed his hair, pulling off a hairpiece to reveal a scraggly, nearly bald head. "I thought as much," she said, tossing it to the floor. Gordon sighed with relief that they weren't going to be shot. He could feel Zera's hands tied to his and stroked her fingers with his own.

"As for you," Tiffany said to Fontana. "I'd like to make you do something totally degrading for my amusement to pay you back, but you'd probably only enjoy it, you pervert."

"Tiffany, please," Fontana begged.

"Stop calling me that; I'm not Tiffany any more. That's a stage name," she barked. "I'm not Tiffany!"

As she reached for the door handle, she turned back to Oscar. "What's your name, by the way? Your real name?"

Oscar Hammerstein's shoulders slumped, and he turned crimson with embarrassment.

"Leonard," he said softly.

"Leonard?" she said incredulously, shaking her head as she left the office, closing the door behind her.

The four captives looked at each other for a moment before struggling to get free. Fontana and Oscar were almost prone on the floor and could not leverage themselves to tug on the pipe, which was firmly in place. Gordon found one end of Zera's knot and worked it until it was loose, and she was free to help him. They pulled the duct tape from their mouths.

"How did you know how to loosen the knot?" she asked.

"Eagle scout," Gordon said quietly. "Had to learn them all." He turned to Oscar and said, "You tie a lousy figure eight, by the way; were you ever a scout?"

"Never made it past Tenderfoot," he said.

With Gordon and Zera now loose from their bonds, Fontana started to implore him to be let go as well.

"Gordon; please understand it wasn't personal. Get me off the hook here and I'll make sure you get a supplement to your teaching fellowship. I can help you."

Gordon looked at him. "You're too ridiculous to even be pathetic," he said, picking up his cell phone from the pile of debris, something Tiffany hadn't noticed in the general commotion of the falling ceiling.

"Don't! Please! I'll write your dissertation for you!" Fontana exclaimed.

Gordon looked at Fontana, and considered how much tedious work that would entail.

"You ARE nuts!"

Gordon fished into his pocket, found Detective Sabatini's card, and called him, leaving his own name and number when the detective's greeting finished.

"If you come to Mandeville Hall, Columbia, we have the crime solved," he said.

Sabatini picked up, cursing at first, but when Gordon told him he had the whole thing on tape, Sabatini said he would call Columbia police to secure the site, and he would be there soon.

Campus police came and taped off the room. A half hour later Sabatini and two uniformed officers arrived. Gordon explained what had happened and played the recording. Sabatini waved his cigar at Gordon and said he could now be prosecuted for breaking and entering, but Gordon waved the keys he had been given by Runcie at him, and Sabatini agreed that perhaps he had the real criminal in custody and the rest could be sorted out.

Sabatini unlocked Fontana and Oscar only to re-cuff them. He let Fontana put his clothes on, but not without staring incredulously at "...the man in purple underpants, the bodybuilder who was crying, the woman reporter badgering him, and the now former suspect in the theft sitting calmly in the professor's chair like the cat who swallowed the canary," as he said in whispered tones on his cell phone to the assistant district attorney he called to tell him to prepare for another arraignment.

The next morning Gordon, Zera, and Harvey went to the police station to hear the detective say that Fontana had confessed; a search warrant obtained had found evidence of other thefts, and the amphora was recovered at the Stanopoulos Gallery.

"He spilled his guts once he knew we had him," Sabatini said. "He pinched the am-fow-ra, as well as many other things from the Penniman, to finance his pursuit of the stripper. The day of the lecture he went to Longstreet's office; Longstreet opened the safe to check on it, suddenly grabbed his chest and keeled over. Fontana realized he had a golden opportunity, carried the vase out in a plastic trash bag, relocked the safe, dragged Longstreet's body to a place behind his desk, took his watch and wallet to make it look like a robbery, and hightailed it to the gallery to give the vase to Stanopoulos who had bought other things from him, and still get back to Columbia in time for his lecture. Stanopoulos apparently owes huge sums to loan sharks for gambling debts, and that is why he became the conduit for stolen property."

"And the rest was to frame me?"

"Everything; the story of the black kid, the package of money Fontana planted, the whole thing."

"And aren't you going to apologize to Gordon for believing all those lies," Zera said with outrage in her voice.

"Sorry, kid. No hard feelings, but we have to do our job."

"That's not an apology!" Zera snapped.

"It's enough for me," Gordon said and shook the detective's hand.

"Do you want to see him? He's got a bail hearing in a few hours and I've got him in a cell downstairs. I can't let you hit him, but if you want to spit on him or something, I'll look the other way. I'll just say I took you down to ID him and you got carried away."

Zera looked at Gordon who nodded yes, and they went downstairs along an ancient brick-lined wall which had been painted over dozens of times in pale green.

Gordon looked at Fontana as he sat, unkempt and scruffy, on a thin mattress.

"How could you do this to me? How could you throw away your whole career so cheaply?"

Fontana hung his head. "I was addicted to a certain kind of love," he croaked in a dry voice. "I'm a victim."

"Herodotus would find that laughable," Gordon replied and walked away.

When they left the police station, the news vans were arriving and Zera said, "I've got to run to finish writing this story. Call me!"

She ran for the sidewalk, hailed a cab, and was gone.

Sabatini said the charges against Gordon were being dropped as they spoke.

"When you arrested me you said if I was innocent, you were Queen Marie of Romania," Gordon reminded him.

Sabatini laughed. "I abdicate the throne, then."

Gordon walked home a free man. The warm air of the August day surrounded him, and he was aware of a great difference in his outlook, indeed of his very self. The past eight weeks had changed him from a hapless, helpless being of a year earlier to a man who had suffered a great injustice, and by wit and daring had overcome it. He thought of the opening lines of the Odyssey: "Andra moi ennepe, mousa polutropon hos molla polla plangthe ; Sing to me muse of a much travelled man who had suffered many wrongs." The student life seemed rather small and trivial to him now. The past few days had given him a rush of adrenalin that made him feel more alive. Even an immense, powerful city like New York had been unable to beat the spirit out of him.

He was, he decided, meant to be a man of action not contemplation. His days with books, aside from pleasure and enlightenment, were over. He had a list of possibilities forming in his mind as he climbed the stairs of his building. Virtue needed a champion, he told himself, and his newly found talents needed an outlet.

He saw Frank Kelley on the landing.

"How are you doing today, son?" the old man asked.

"Never better, "Gordon said. "Just you wait and see."

XII

"Caelum, non animum, mutant
qui trans mare currunt."

-HORACE

("Those who cross the sea change their
environment, not themselves.")

THE THIRD WEEK OF AUGUST brought Gordon's complete exoneration. Having established his innocence by means of Fontana's unmasking, Columbia was quick to reinstate him to his former position and even offer payment of lost wages if he agreed not to sue. The university attorney drafted a letter which Gordon brought to Harvey Knippelman. Zera, who accompanied him in the full flush of her own triumph as the investigative reporter who first broke the story, sat and smoked a cigarette jubilantly while Harvey read the proposed settlement.

"It's chump change, Harvey said contemptuously as he tossed the paper down on his desk. "Sue the university for two hundred thousand. They made no efforts to consider anything except the word of Fontana, their employee, who had you suspended and set in the dock for crimes which might have included murder."

Gordon shook his head. "That's not what I had in mind. I have some other demands that are more important. I want you to come with me while I make them an offer they can't refuse."

Zera stood up from her chair and smiled. "The young Vito Corleone," she said.

An appointment was made for the next day and Gordon, Zera, and Harvey went to the president's office where Sterling Vaughner Pew, Jr., Dean Aimer, and the assistant legal counsel Josh Stearn sat waiting for what they thought would be a seven-figure defamation suit.

A silver tea service was set on the side table, and a white-jacketed waiter brought them pastries on a platter, and set out milk and lemons in matching vessels, all bearing the crest of Columbia University. When the waiter left, the business of the day began.

"We're very sorry, Mr. Bauer," Stearn began.

"Gordon, we are truly sorry," the president said, wringing his hands in effusive servility.

"I know, and I accept your apology," Gordon answered, "but there are a few other things I need as well."

They cringed as he continued.

"First a monetary settlement for eleven thousand dollars, which is what I lost in wages and what I owe Mr. Knippelman."

They sighed with a bit of relief and Gordon continued.

"Second: I want two box seats near the field by the first base side for the Yankees-White Sox game on September 6th . It's a Saturday afternoon game, and I'll need a limo to pick up me and my neighbor, Mr. Kelley, take us to the stadium, wait, and bring us back."

The president scribbled a note. Gordon had no doubt he could get the tickets with a single phone call.

"And third: there is a playground at 135th Street. For years there has been a plan to name it after Edward Wyatt, an army sergeant who was killed in Iraq. All that needs to be done is put up a plaque and have a ceremony his mother can attend. It needs some cleaning up, asphalt patched and sealed, repainted lines for the basketball court, the usual."

The president wrote some more.

"And?" Sterling Vaughner Pew, Jr. said, ready for more extortionate demands than had already been enumerated.

"That's all."

"Gordon!" Harvey exclaimed.

Gordon waved him off. "No, that is all I want. The money I would like soon, the baseball game on the sixth, and the playground before the end of September."

"Well, I don't know if things can work that fast," Dean Aimer huffed.

"Are you willing to sign a release if we agree to this?" Josh Stearn asked.

"Absolutely," Gordon answered, rising and buttoning his suit jacket.

"Then it will be done," the president announced with a thump of his knuckles on the desk.

"I don't know if the city will be able to...", Aimer protested.

"Christ, Henry, we employ a thousand buildings and groundskeepers. They could rebuild that playground in a day if we turned them loose on it. Tell the city we will get all the work done at the university's expense, including the plaque. I might not be able to change higher education, but like Pharaoh, I can order something to be built!"

Gordon, Zera, and Harvey left with the attorney still shaking his head. "I could have gotten you twenty-five thou then and there!"

"I know, but I don't need it as much as I need those other things."

Harvey left for downtown, while Zera and Gordon went for a walk in Riverside Park. The clear blue sky and cooler air gave a hint of autumn, and Gordon held his shoulders back and his head high.

"My story on the case has put me in Darwin's good graces," she said. "He wants to give me more space and freedom for my columns and investigative reporting."

Gordon suddenly remembered something Zera had said back in the beginning.

"You had the case solved a long time ago," he said. "You told me the culprit was white, an academic with a trick up his sleeve, and unstable due to an obsessive fixation on something."

"I did?" Zera said. "Well, maybe I did, but I don't remember half the things that come out of my mouth."

They went to a vegetarian place nearby and ordered miso soup, tofu, salad, and brown rice, and Gordon told her he thought the whole adventure could be an ancient Greek play or maybe something by Shakespeare.

"There you go again," Zera said. "Your only point of reference is dead, white European males. You don't bother your head with how that whole tradition has dominated the humanities and omitted the histories of women, sexual minorities, and people of color."

"That is what I hear all the time now by history and literature professors."

"So maybe they're right?"

"No, overcorrecting," Gordon said. "That is part of the story, and they have made it the whole story. It isn't a perspective, it's an ideology. Only the classicists seem to be holdouts."

"You say the Athenians invented democracy," Zera began, but…"

"…but they owned slaves, too, I know." Gordon replied, finishing her sentence. "The ancient world had its dark side undeniably."

"Then why do you still hold to this conservative, privileged, white male view?"

"Why are you so sure I do?"

"You likely vote Republican," she said, almost hissing it out.

"For the record, I would have voted for Obama if I'd been old enough," Gordon said.

She paused. "Because he's from Illinois, too," she replied, sticking her tongue out playfully.

"Eat your tofu," he said.

The next day Gordon went for his army physical and tests. At a drab military building surrounded by young men, some of whom appeared eager, others resigned, and some just bewildered, they gave him a battery of written tests, and an interview, and after a dismal lunch of fish sticks, peas, and mashed potato at a nearby diner with an army meal voucher, a physical examination. Lined up with a hundred others in just their undershorts, doctors came by and checked their heart rates, looked into ears, noses, and mouths, examined feet, and finally had them drop their shorts for a hernia exam, then turn around and bend over.

"USDA prime meat," the man next to Gordon mumbled under his breath.

They were told to get dressed and call the recruiter they had spoken with at the beginning. Gordon called the sergeant late that afternoon and he seemed delighted.

"Maybe you were hoping for rangers or combat infantry, Mr. Bauer, but you seem to have an unusual skill at learning languages. The army always needs people like you, and if you enlist, we can offer you a very unusual chance to take your skills to the next level, most likely in intelligence."

Gordon said he would think it over, that his situation was a bit different, but that he was still interested. He called Zera when he got home, but didn't mention the army. They chatted and agreed to meet that evening, and had dinner three nights in a row at an Afghan, Vietnamese, and Tongan restaurant respectively, and in a moment of tenderness and three glasses of wine, she invited him to her parents' house on Long Island that coming Sunday for a meal and a swim in the pool. The Alperts were just back from Europe, and Zera's brother Stephen, his wife Stacey, and their two-year-old son Jacob would all be there.

On Sunday they navigated a rental car through the traffic of the Long Island Expressway to Great Neck. The Alperts were cordial and wanted to hear the whole story of the stolen amphora. Gordon began, working up to the finale, when a loud crash and yelp interrupted him. Jacob had overturned a bowl of applesauce from his highchair onto the Alperts' hapless terrier Duncan.

Once the yelping, crying, and screaming had subsided, Gordon finished the story. Mr. Alpert asked Gordon about his academic work and seemed pleased, but Gordon knew any sign of approbation from Zera's father would ruin any chance of his with her, for she was a woman for whom parental approval was the kiss of death.

Zera was silent as they drove back to Manhattan, and Gordon

knew, just as his summer adventure was over, so were things with her. The next day she met him for lunch at the Checkerboard, a bistro on Broadway near Columbia with a black and white motif on everything from the tablecloths to the ceiling.

As if she had rehearsed the lines, Zera began to speak deliberately. "Gordon, you're really sweet and nice, and I've had the most exciting summer of my life, but we really don't have much in common, you know. I don't want to hurt your feelings, but you'd be better off with someone quite unlike me."

She waited for his reply, and he looked at her intently.

"I know all that," he said and smiled.

She seemed relieved. "I thought you would be unhappy when I told you."

"I was unhappy the last few weeks every time I came to the same conclusion, but then I saw it was the truth and I became un-unhappy."

"I'm not sure I understand," she said.

"I'm not sure I do, either, except to say that I think this summer I finally grew up."

They finished lunch and paid the check. On the way out he said, "Columbia has come through on the playground. The dedication is Saturday, September 13th. Would you do me the honor of coming with me?"

"Of course," she said.

"Good, because I'll be leaving town right after that."

"Leaving town; doesn't school start soon?"

"Oh, it does, "Gordon said, "but I'm not going back to school. I'm not cut out for academia. The night I broke into Mandeville Hall

I realized I had spent enough time studying and contemplating life. Now it's time to have one."

"You're not becoming a cat burglar, are you?"

"Close; a criminal investigator."

"Go on," she said with amusement.

"You can't start there, so I'm joining the army first. I tested so high on language ability that they're going to send me to language school in Monterey, California, then on to intelligence. But that's just my first stop. After my hitch, I plan on joining the FBI to focus on things like art thefts and forgeries. When I know what I need to know, I'm going to start my own agency."

She gasped in mock astonishment. "Sounds like you have the next twenty years planned."

"I've researched this; art theft is very big, while law enforcement and insurance companies are trying to catch up."

"You know as a radical, I detest police and military people on principle, but I guess I am going to have to make an exception for you."

They stopped on the sidewalk and Zera said she had to browse some things on child labor in a bookstore nearby. "I'm thinking of doing a story on third-world working conditions."

Gordon smiled, thinking of her being ten thousand miles away on one of her quests.

"Oh, Zera," he said quietly as a tear came to his eye.

"Gordo," she replied, as if it would be followed by something, but instead she took a deep breath and hugged him as they stood there on Broadway at West 107th Street. She stepped back, walked away, turned to wave, and then crossed Broadway toward the bookstore.

Gordon stood where he was and watched as she eventually disappeared into the crowd.

Gordon was told that since he had completed eight courses, he would be granted the M.A. degree, which made him feel at least his living in New York for a year would not be a completely blank line on his resume.

The day of the baseball game, the mail carrier brought a package. It was a copy of *The Histories* by Herodotus, leather-bound, with an inscription from Zera which he couldn't decipher, but cherished nonetheless.

The limousine arrived before noon, and Gordon helped Frank into the back seat where champagne on ice waited for them.

"Can I just have a beer at the park?' Frank said, and Gordon assured him he could.

The limo went to a special gate and an usher brought them to their seats, wiping them down with a towel. Gordon gave the attendant a five-dollar tip from the spending money Columbia had provided for the day. Frank's eyes lit up when he saw how close they were to the field.

"Jeez, kid. Great seats!"

It was a perfect September day, and Gordon relished the green of the grass, the crack of the bat, and the elation of the crowd, although unfortunately the cracking and the cheering were mostly about the Yankees who beat his beloved White Sox 7 to 2. But they saw a triple play, had cold beer and hot dogs, and were whisked back to Manhattan like royalty. Gordon felt a wave of affability wash over him from the half a cup of beer he drank, and the world seemed in harmony as he watched the late-day sun fold in behind the buildings on Amsterdam Avenue.

Gordon packed up his apartment, shipped some things home, and prepared to leave New York for basic training after a short visit with his parents in Illinois. The last event was the dedication of the playground to Alma's son.

A surprise call at three A.M. one morning woke him up with a start. It was his former neighbor Ali, who was in Ululistan.

"Turn on CNN, my friend; we have won."

Gordon turned on the television and saw Ali and his cousins atop a tank in the Ululibad city square. The khaki-clad woman war correspondent was interviewing the rebel leaders as celebratory gunfire could be heard in the background.

"We have won, and some thanks to you. Khalil and Hamid send their hellos. I am to be deputy minister of transportation, my friend. Isn't that funny? From driving a New York taxicab to running the airports and railroads!"

"You will need a new suit from London," Gordon advised.

"No, we will dress as the ordinary people," he shouted as static engulfed their words.

Gordon wished him well and then their connection was suddenly snapped.

On Saturday, September 13th, Gordon and Zera went to the 135th Street playground for the dedication ceremony. A bronze plaque, in the end paid for and designed by one of the veterans' organizations to commemorate Alma's son, had been set in stone at the park's entrance. The mayor and some of the city council, community leaders, and school children turned out. A minister gave an invocation and a high school band played *The Star Spangled Banner*. Alma wept, both from happiness and unhappiness, but was also filled with a look of dignity and triumph.

Zera had a photographer from *The Twelfth Street Liberator* there and he took a picture of Gordon and Alma by the plaque which read, "In Memory of Sergeant First Class Edwin D. Wyatt, Jr., U.S. Army, who once played here. He served his country with honor and gave his life in Iraq for our freedom."

"I can't agree politically with the plaque, of course," Zera began pontificating when Alma had stepped away.

"I know you can't," Gordon interrupted, "so just enjoy her moment."

Zera was chastened by the rebuke and took Gordon's hand as they walked around to inspect the new plantings.

"Well, this is so long," he finally said when they were back at the entrance.

"Keep in touch," she said, kissing his cheek. She paused and looked at him for a moment before adding, "I know I can be blunt and maladroit, but take this as a compliment: when you shed your angst and grow up, you will be an amazing person, Gordon Bauer, and I think you're halfway there."

He smiled, kissed her cheek, and turned to walk back to his flat to get ready for his flight the next morning.

Traveling over the eastern states was pleasant while looking at the earth from a high vantage point. Once on the ground in Chicago, he rented a car and drove to his parents' house in Bellflower, admiring the cornfields after the harvest, plain and solemn in their barrenness. Things were pretty much the same except for a new strip mall where Timmerman's Grain and Feed store had been. Gordon would have a week before reporting to the army and wanted to assure his parents he had not lost his mind.

"The army was good for me," Gordon's father had said. He had been in for two years, spending most of his time as a company clerk in Texas typing forms.

Mr. and Mrs. Bauer noticed the change in Gordon, his new self-confidence in bearing and demeanor. They asked about the woman in New York he had told them about, but he said that was over.

"Oh," his mother said.

"It's all right. I don't think we were compatible. Even figuring out where and what to eat was a challenge. I realized a happy marriage is dependent on only one thing."

"And that is…," Mr. Bauer said.

"Deciding what to have for dinner. Once that is resolved, everything else falls into place."

Gordon phoned Father Kottmeyer to tell him he had left school and was not going to be a professor after all.

The priest listened, and at the end of Gordon's soliloquy said, "Dream your own dreams, Gordon, that is the only lesson the classics teach that is worth knowing. Gnothi se auton; know thyself."

On Gordon's last night with his parents, his mother cooked his favorite fried chicken with corn on the cob, potato salad, and chocolate cake for dessert. As Gordon ate his second helping of cake while the autumn sun slipped into the horizon, the deep, dark chocolate frosting sent ecstatic sensations along neural pathways from his taste buds to his brain. He thought of mid-western girls with round, fulsome breasts and having time to read what he wanted rather than what he was assigned. These sensations he enjoyed most: chocolate, sex, and good books began to assuage his melancholy over Zera, ancient amphoras, and the lost-forever romanticism he had attached to New York.

Printed in the United States
by Baker & Taylor Publisher Services

Printed in the United States
by Baker & Taylor Publisher Services